DOG TREATS AND DEATH

A TALKING DOG COZY MYSTERY

HEYWOOD HOUNDS COZY MYSTERIES BOOK 1

CARLY WINTER

Edited by
DIVAS AT WORK EDITING
Cover By
COVEREDBYMELINDA.COM

WESTWARD PUBLISHING / CARLY FALL, LLC

ABOUT THIS BOOK

He's had a troubled past... but is he a killer?

When Gina Dunner's brother, Vic, is accused of murdering his ex-girlfriend, Gina isn't surprised. Living the life of a womanizing ranch hand with questionable friends and a lifetime of bad choices had to catch up with him at some point.

After the Sheriff announces she has the right man, Vic vehemently denies the murder. When he begs Gina to help prove his innocence, she attempts to puts her doubts aside, despite him being the last one to see the woman alive. She and her rescue mutt, Daisy—a sweet, yet sassy, talking dog—start sniffing around into their own investigation.

Will Gina and Daisy stumble onto the truth to exonerate Vic, or will the killer come for Gina next?

Journey with amateur sleuths, Gina and Daisy, through the twists and turns of "Dog Treats and Death," a tale of family, betrayal, and the enduring bond between a woman and her extraordinary canine companion.

CHAPTER 1

"WILL YOU HELP ME?"

My older brother's voice coming through the phone didn't carry the usual swagger of the self-assured man I knew, and whose actions tested the patience of saints. In fact, there was a hint of desperation. I'd be anxious, too, if I were him. The sheriff had just accused him of murdering his ex-girlfriend.

"Fine. I'm on my way, Vic," I grumbled. The last thing I wanted to do was be involved in Vic's drama. But, when I'd been locked up and accused of killing someone, he'd come to visit almost every day, bringing me a breath of insanity and usually a couple of laughs.

As children, Vic had always been by my side, protecting me. Like the time a kid stole my bike at school. My brother had hunted him down, exchanged some harsh words with him, and returned my bike. Or when we'd been messing around in the woods and I'd fallen and sprained my ankle. He'd carried me out. As adults, he irritated me beyond measure with his panache for bad choices in every aspect of his life because I was the one he always called on to help him right his wrongs.

Like I didn't have enough to do.

I drove down Comfort Road, the main street in the idyllic little town of Heywood, Arizona, located in the mountains near Sedona. On my left stood the storefronts, or the downtown area, as most of the locals referred to it. Beyond the buildings, a river meandered through thick forest. To my right, streets cut up through the trees to the residential areas. I'd lived in Heywood my whole life, and I'd considered leaving more than once. Yet, I always ended up staying.

"Do you think he killed that woman?" a soft voice asked from the back seat. I glanced into the rearview mirror to find big brown eyes staring at me from a brown and white furry face—my rescue dog, Daisy.

Yes, speaking to the dog had been very weird at first, and I'd even questioned my sanity. But now, six months after the accident that had caused me to hear her voice, I'd just accepted that my brain had been rewired when I'd knocked my head on the tree branch while chasing the little turd through the snow. She'd spent two nights out in the bitter cold winter air, and the other rescuers and I were determined to make sure she didn't have to attempt to survive another.

"Probably not," I mumbled.

"Probably not?"

"I'm hoping not," I said. "Vic likes trouble." Although, I had a hard time imagining what kind of trouble would lead to him hurting a woman.

Vic liking trouble—that was the understatement of the year. Bar fights, speeding on his motorcycle, and selling drugs were a few of his favorite extracurricular activities.

"You're driving kind of fast, Gina. Who do you think you are? Mario Andretti?"

Daisy didn't like my tendency to get to where I needed to go as quickly as possible. Hmm… maybe I shouldn't be so judgmental of my brother.

"Sorry," I said. "I'm just worried about Vic."

"But I thought you didn't like him," she said.

Did I like my brother? Sometimes. Did I love him? Yes. "It's complicated," I sighed. And a situation I didn't feel like explaining to my talking dog.

Vic worked at the Diamond Ranch, a place about six miles out of town. The sun beat down relentlessly on the summer day and once I got out of traffic, I opened the windows.

"This kind of feels like a hairdryer in my face," Daisy yelled as she stuck her snout out the window. "But I love it!"

With a smile, I pressed my foot on the accelerator and hoped the cops had something better to do than give me a ticket on an open road with little traffic.

Minutes later, I slowed as I pulled onto the long, tree-lined, dirt road leading to Diamond Ranch. After a quarter mile, we rounded the bend. A large brown house with green trim and a matching barn came into view, along with acres of green grass and dozens of horses. The Diamond Ranch specialized in breeding Arabian and quarter horses. Well, that's what Vic had told me. Personally, I couldn't tell the difference from one to the other. They all had four legs and some were prettier than others.

"What are those?" Daisy asked. "Big dogs?"

I chuckled and shook my head.

"Horses. I take it you've never seen one before?"

"No, I haven't. They're huge! And they smell weird."

As I pulled up to the main house, I realized the reason I hadn't received a ticket on my ride over was because the cops were all at the ranch. They stood outside an arena where a lone figure covered in a white sheet lay in the middle.

"That's not a horse," I muttered.

"I think you're right," Daisy said. "That's definitely a dead human. Is that the one Vic murdered?"

"No, Daisy! He didn't kill anyone!"

"Well, you've made it clear you have your doubts."

I rolled down the back window fully so Daisy wouldn't get hot, then exited the car. As I approached the group of people, it was easy to spot Vic. His huge frame towered over almost everyone. I also noted Sheriff Mallory Richards, Deputy Trevor Hutchinson, and the owner of the ranch, Roger Wagner, were present. Tall and thin,

Roger wore a black cowboy hat, just as he had the first time we'd become acquainted a few years ago during the ranch Christmas party Vic had asked me to attend with him. I hoped Wagner didn't remember me. I had spilled a glass of red wine down his wife's white dress and onto the white carpet. Man, had she been angry. Then, despite my apologies, she'd called me a bunch of names, which caused me to say a few things I shouldn't have, and I'd been escorted from the party.

Vic nodded in my direction as I advanced then Mallory turned to me, narrowing her gaze. I'd known Trevor Hutchinson almost my whole life, and he simply smiled, giving me a quick wave. Wagner barely gave me a second glance.

"What are you doing here?" Mallory asked when I got within hearing distance. Short and muscular with black hair, I often thought she did more harm than good in her position, but no one would challenge her in the polls, so she continued to be elected.

"Just visiting my brother," I replied, then pointed to the figure lying in the middle of the arena. "Looks like you have a problem though, Sheriff." I smiled innocently. "How long are you going to let the poor thing lie there?"

I didn't meet Roger Wagner's gaze but felt his stare on me.

"Am I supposed to believe you've just turned up to visit your brother in the middle of a murder investigation?" Mallory shot back.

"How did she die?" I asked, ignoring her question.

"It looks like a blow to the head," Trevor replied.

"So, you don't actually know if it was murder," I said. "She could've been kicked by a horse, right?"

"Don't think so," Trevor said. "There weren't any horses in the arena when she was found."

"Who found her?" I asked.

"I did," Roger said. "Aren't you that

woman who spilled red wine on my carpet?"

"And your wife, sir," Vic added. "She also spilled it on your wife. That's my sister, Gina."

I shot him a glare. He asked me to come help him then threw me under the bus. Typical Vic.

"Look, you need to leave right now," Mallory hissed. "Get off this *private* property."

"Great idea," I said. "I'll take my brother with me."

"You will not!" she yelled as her cheeks reddened, her voice oozing annoyance. It was so easy to get under her skin.

"Why?" I asked innocently. "Is he under arrest? Or are you still in the middle of your investigation, as Trevor just mentioned, and you don't have any evidence to hold my brother?"

Trevor rolled his eyes while Vic's satisfied grin spread from ear to ear.

"She's right, Sheriff," Roger said. "I'd

like to get poor Phoebe taken care of first and foremost. The rest can wait."

All of us turned to look at the body. I gasped in horror when I realized Daisy had jumped from the car and was now sniffing around the dead woman.

"Whose dog is that?!" Mallory yelled. "It's going to contaminate the area!"

Crud. Mother of all things holy. That dang dog had her nose to the ground as she circled the body. "Daisy!" I yelled. "Get over here!"

I began to crawl through the bars, but Mallory grabbed the back of my shirt and pulled me away from them.

"Daisy!" I screamed. "Get your little butt over here right now or get back to the car this very instant!"

She glanced up at me, tilted her head to the side, then turned her gaze to the body once again.

"I mean it!" I yelled. "If you don't get back into that car by the count of three, you won't get to sleep on the bed tonight. One! Two!"

She took off toward the vehicle and sailed through the open window with ease.

"I swear that dog understood every word you just said," Trevor muttered.

If he only knew, which he never would. No one could know my secret.

While Mallory railed on about her contaminated crime scene, an ambulance emerged from the tree-lined driveway and drove over to us. As they exited the vehicle and Mallory turned her attention to them, it seemed like the perfect time to gather Vic and leave.

I met his gaze and motioned him to follow me. He took two steps and Trevor grabbed his arm. "Don't leave the area, Vic," he warned. "Whether you did this or not, the sheriff is going to want a word or two with you."

He nodded and we hurried over to my car.

I sighed as I slid into the driver's seat, then shot a glare at Daisy through the rearview mirror.

"Don't be mad, Gina," she said, wagging her tail as she licked the side of my face. "I just wanted to see who had been around that person."

"Did you smell anything?" I whispered as Vic opened the passenger door.

"Yes!"

Vic entered and laid his head against the headrest while Daisy sniffed him.

As I started the car, I met her gaze in the mirror again.

"I smelled Vic," she said. "And two other people, but I don't know who."

Glancing over at my brother, I asked, "Why do they think you killed Phoebe?"

"Because I was the last one to see her."

I accelerated down the tree-lined driveway to the highway. "When was that?"

"Last night," he replied.

"I thought you two had broken up," I said.

"We did, but she needed my help."

"With what?" I asked.

For a mile or so, we drove in silence and I realized he didn't want to share anything with me about his talk with Phoebe the prior evening. Finally, I said, "Vic, if you want me to help you, I need to know the details regarding what she wanted to speak to you about."

He sighed. "I know."

"And we should discuss who would want her dead," I said. Hopefully, the list was long. Since Vic had been the last to see her alive and Daisy had smelled him next to the body, things weren't looking good for my brother.

CHAPTER 2

As we pulled into the driveway at my house, Daisy started barking. The other dogs answered from inside, their little faces showing through the living room window.

"How many mutts do you have now?" Vic asked, studying my humble abode, a white house with blue trim. I kept the front yard pretty basic—a swath of grass and some rose bushes against the house. The backyard I also kept as simple as I could with grass and a few trees. I'd fully admit I cared more about my dogs than the esthetics of my home.

"Three, including Daisy," I replied.

We exited the car and Daisy followed, sniffing at Vic's boots. I was worried that she smelled him around Phoebe's body, but I had to hold faith that he was telling me the truth and they'd talked the prior night.

"Did anyone have a guess how long she'd been dead?" I asked.

Vic shrugged. "Not that anyone told me."

I opened the front door and the two other dogs greeted us. The small white terrier and the fluffy brown chow quieted down when they saw Vic, but immediately sniffed around his feet.

"You remember Sing," I said, setting my keys on the entry table and pointing at the chow. "And the other one is Banshee."

"Banshee?" Vic asked. "How did you come up with that one?"

"Don't ask," I replied. I wasn't about to explain that the dog had given herself the name and Daisy had informed me of the new moniker. "Do you want some water?"

"Whisky, if you have it," he said, leaning over to stroke my rescues.

"It's ten in the morning, Vic."

"And Phoebe's dead, Gina. I'm a little shook up about everything, so if you have the whisky, just pour it and don't lecture me."

With a huff, I strode into the kitchen and pulled a bottle out from above the stove. I couldn't remember the last time I'd drank any of the amber liquid. Could it go bad?

"We'll find out," I muttered as I poured him a glass. He sat down at my kitchen table and I set it down in front of him. Then I opened the back door and told the dogs to go outside.

"Tell me what happened," I said, taking a seat across from him. As he sipped his drink, I studied my brother. Working in the sun had lined his tan face, but he was still as handsome as ever with his strong jaw and high cheekbones peeking out from under his thick brown beard. He sighed and ran a hand through his unmanageable curly hair. More than once, I'd wondered if we were truly related because we looked so different.

I tucked a lock of blonde hair behind my ear as I stared Vic down, waiting for him to speak.

After finishing his whisky, he stood, grabbed the bottle from the counter, then sat back down and poured another. "Phoebe came to me yesterday afternoon and said she had a problem and needed some advice. She asked if we could meet later in the evening."

"What was the problem?" I asked. "And why was she coming to you? If I remember right, you cheated on her and she dumped you."

He chuckled and shook his head. "You were never one to mince words, Gina."

"What part did I get wrong?"

"Nothing. I was a jerk and she left me."

"Okay, so why was she coming to you? If I try to put myself in her shoes, I wouldn't go to you for the time of day, let alone help in solving a problem."

He slowly spun his glass in his fingers. "That's a good question. I don't know why she came to me, but she did. We did remain friendly after I screwed everything up, though."

I rolled my eyes. "Vic, she slashed your tires."

"Well, after that she cooled down. We agreed that if we had to work together, there wasn't any reason we couldn't be civil."

"So, what was this big thing she needed advice on?"

He stared at his glass for a long moment. "She was having an affair with Roger."

For a second, I blanked. "Roger?" Then it hit me. "Roger?! As in the owner of Diamond Ranch, Roger Wagner?!"

Vic nodded. "The one and only."

"And he's married," I muttered, shaking my head. If there was one thing I detested, it was infidelity—having been in a short marriage where it was prevalent had left a bad taste in my mouth. In fact, the only good thing that had come out of the venture was my son, Jacob. Just thinking about him caused my chest to ache. Yes, he was living his best life at college, but I missed my kid.

Back to Vic. Maybe his problems were the distraction I needed from my own loneliness. "So what was the big issue?"

"She wanted to break it off, but she didn't want to lose her job."

"Do you think he'd do that?" I asked. "Fire her because she didn't want to sleep with him any longer?"

Vic tossed back his whisky and shrugged. "I don't know."

"Who else would want her dead?" I asked.

Daisy barked at the back door. I stood to let her and the other dogs in. After they each had some water, Sing exited for the living room while Banshee took her place by the feeding bowl so she could get the next meal first. She didn't seem to understand she'd eaten mere hours ago. Daisy curled up on top of my feet under the table.

"I don't know, Gina," Vic sighed.

"Come on, Vic. Think! They're talking about taking you in for murder!"

"We don't even know if she was killed!" Vic yelled, slamming his hand down on the table. "She could've been kicked by a horse!"

"How does that work when there wasn't a horse in the arena?" I asked, ignoring his outburst.

"Tell him we don't like yelling in our house," Daisy said. "It makes me nervous." I reached down and gave her head a quick stroke, hoping to reassure her that overall, my brother was harmless, but he could be loud.

"Maybe she was working with a horse and she was kicked, then someone came along and didn't see her in the arena after dark, but took the horse away."

"Why would she work with a horse after dark?" I asked.

Vic shrugged. "I know we recently sold a couple of Arabians. Maybe she was doing some extra training with them to make sure they'd mind their manners in their new home."

After dark would mean that she'd have the lights on, which indicated that someone would see her lying in the middle of the arena if they came to fetch the horse.

"Perhaps the lights were on a timer or something?" I asked.

"Yeah, they are. They're set to go off at ten, just in case we forget to shut them off."

Okay, so maybe his theory of her being kicked by a horse held some water. I would think a medical examiner would find proof of that. Maybe a horse hoof print on her forehead or something...

"Who told Sheriff Mallory you were the last person to see Phoebe?" I asked.

"That, I don't know. I was mucking out

the barns in the back of the property like I do every morning. Roger came in and told me the cops needed to talk to me. I went over to the arena and found the police and Roger staring at Phoebe. They started asking me a bunch of questions and I quickly realized I was in a bit of trouble. I excused myself to the bathroom. That's when I called you."

But I wasn't sure what I was supposed to do. I glanced at my brother again and noted tears in his eyes. Goodness. The only time I'd seen him cry was when our mother had told us she was going out for groceries and she'd never come back. I'd been four and he'd been almost ten. I remembered he'd blamed himself for it because he'd refused to unload the dishwasher and told our mom she was fat right before she left.

"I loved Phoebe," he said. "I screwed up our relationship, like I screw up everything, but I did love her, and I'd never hurt her, Gina."

My throat closed at this show of emotion. Like my father, Vic had always been good at expressing only one sentiment: anger. The rest of it stayed neatly tucked away.

How did I help this big buffoon breaking down at my kitchen table?

I cleared my throat. In my past experiences with the sheriff, her investigation methods were lazy and she liked easy answers. If she had already tossed around the idea that Vic was a murderer when we weren't really sure if Phoebe had been killed, then I had to assume she wouldn't change her tactics. I'd sat in jail a few days when my ex-husband turned up dead in my nail salon, File It Away, and the sheriff had arrested me for it. Suddenly, the way to help my brother became clear. If Phoebe had been killed, we had to be ready to steer the sheriff in another direction, away from Vic. I had to flood Mallory with options on who else the killer could be.

"Who else would want her dead?" I

asked again. "And this time, think about it."

After a long moment, he said, "If she'd told Roger she wanted to end their relationship, maybe he lost it and killed her."

"Okay, that's good," I replied. "A crime of passion. Who else?"

"Maybe his wife?" Vic suggested. "Maybe she found out about the affair and *she* killed Phoebe."

I nodded, then stood and grabbed a piece of paper and pen from my junk drawer. I loved lists, so I sat down and noted our suspects. "Another crime of passion," I muttered. "But of passionate hatred for sleeping with her husband."

"Chase Thomas was pretty upset about Phoebe getting her recent promotion," Vic said. "He told her to watch her back."

I glanced up from my paper. "You heard him say that?"

"Yeah. He's been at Diamond Ranch for ten years, while Phoebe's been there seven. Chase thought he should've gotten the promotion, not her."

"Was he right?"

Vic shrugged. "Yeah, probably. I didn't know she was sleeping with Roger when it happened. I just figured she'd out-performed him. Now I can't help but wonder if it was her performance between the sheets that got her moved up."

I wrote down Chase's name. So far, we had three really good suspects. "Anyone else?"

Placing his elbows on the table and his head in his hands, he moaned. "Dang it. I should've seen this coming."

"What's that?"

"Debbie Towerhall."

"What about her?" I asked. Debbie Towerhall was trouble with a capital T. A homewrecker who'd had more problems with the law than Vic.

"I was dating her for a bit after Phoebe dumped me."

Gross. He may as well been swimming in sewage, as far as I was concerned. "Oh, man, Vic. That's awful and a new low for you. Did you get tested for STD's?"

"She's not that bad," he mumbled.

"Yes, she is," I said, shaking my head. "The woman is a walking Petri dish. I can't believe you slept with her."

"I broke it off a couple weeks ago."

"Why?"

"Phoebe and I were getting along well at work and I hoped to get back together. I told Debbie that."

"That was a mistake," I muttered while writing her name down.

"I know. I was trying to do the right thing."

"Didn't she stab her last boyfriend who left her?" I asked.

"Yeah, but she didn't kill him."

"Small blessings for him."

"She did spend some time in the slammer for it, though."

I exhaled loudly and crossed my arms over my chest. What a mess. At least I felt confident that we had plenty of other suspects besides my brother, and Debbie moved to the top of the list, especially with her past. "Maybe this time, she didn't go after her boyfriend for revenge, but instead, she killed the woman you were leaving her for."

"Maybe," he muttered, pouring more whisky. "Maybe."

CHAPTER 3

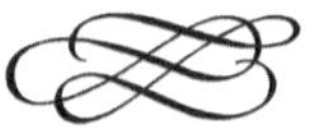

VIC PASSED out on my couch, snoring loudly. Apparently, Sing had decided he needed consoling, because the big fluff ball had curled up on his legs. I watched the two for a moment. Maybe Vic should adopt Sing? Would I *allow* him to adopt the dog? My brother often had trouble taking care of himself and I didn't know if I trusted him with Sing, even though the canine was pretty chill and liked to sleep most of the time. In fact, he may have been the laziest dog I'd ever rescued. I didn't even bother with walks any longer be-cause after a quarter mile, he'd lay down and wouldn't get up unless I started heading back toward the house. Maybe they were a match? With a sigh, I headed down the hall to get to work with Daisy trotting behind me.

After I'd kicked my husband out many years ago, I became a single mother. I'd worked my tail off to provide for my son. For a while, I slugged away at the town paper, and began ghostwriting on the side. When my side gig became more profitable than my job, I stuck with that. I'd also gotten my license and opened a nail salon called File It Away. Although I was only open a couple times a week, I enjoyed my work there. The town of Heywood was surrounded by farms and the women who worked them weren't that interested in pretty fingernails, but they did love a good pedicure. They also liked to gossip, and I enjoyed listening. Due to the limited hours I kept, my store was always full. That's where I got the *real* news of what was going on in town.

I stopped at Jacob's room and stood in

the middle of it for a long moment. After dropping him off to college a few weeks ago, the feeling of utter loneliness had fallen around me like a black cloud. It had been the two of us for so long. Sure I was happy he'd received a full ride scholarship and that he was spreading his wings, but he'd been my buddy for so long, it was hard to have him gone.

"I miss him, too, Gina." I glanced down at Daisy sitting at my feet.

"He's only an hour away," I said. "Maybe we should go visit."

"I love riding in the car!" Her tail wagged as she stared up at me.

"Yes, you do," I replied, reaching down and giving her a quick scratch behind the ears. "Now, let's go into the bedroom and you can tell me about your sniff session around poor Phoebe."

She followed me down the hall to the master bedroom and I shut the door behind us. With Sing passed out on the couch with Vic and Banshee waiting to be fed, I figured we'd have a few moments to ourselves.

After I stepped over the three dog beds, I sat down at my desk. Daisy perched herself on the corner of the bed closest to me.

I fired up my computer, then turned to the dog. "So tell me what you were doing while you were being a bad dog."

"Trying to help you," she said.

Her tongue lolled out the side of her mouth while her tail swished from side to side. I never saw her mouth move when we had conversations, so I often questioned my own sanity. If her mouth didn't move, then that meant I was having the discussion in my head, right? And if that were the case, it probably meant I had something wrong with me or I was certifiable. That was something I'd rather not think about, so I just enjoyed my conversations with the dog.

"You said you smelled Vic by Phoebe's body," I said. "Did you mean like on the dirt? Or where?"

"On her hand."

I nodded. "He's said he talked to her earlier that night."

"Were they holding hands?" Daisy asked.

"Maybe," I shrugged. "Who knows. What else did you find out?"

"Horses stink."

"Yes, they can, but let's concentrate on the human smells. Anyone else that you may have recognized?"

"I don't think so. You didn't give me a lot of time to really track anything."

"How do you know you smelled Vic, then?"

"Because he's been around here before. I remember what he smells like, and I caught the scent on Phoebe."

"Do you think you could've smelled someone else?"

"Maybe two people." She yawned and stretched out on the bed. "But I don't know them."

It was too bad I hadn't realized what Daisy was up to when she'd jumped from the car. If so, I would've called her over and had her take a whiff of Roger as well.

"I think I need a nap," she announced.

"You and me both," I muttered as she shut her eyes.

I turned to my computer and took a deep breath as I hit the email icon and waited for my messages to populate. Scanning them, I found my water bill was due, I had a couple of emails from people I did some writing for, and that was about it, except for the one asking me if I wanted to join a dating site for senior citizens.

"I'm not even fifty," I mumbled.

"Almost," Daisy reminded me. "Just a couple more years."

I glanced over my shoulder at my canine. She stared at me with one eye slightly open and her tail wagging lazily. "You're a funny one, Daisy. Really funny."

"I know," she whispered.

Dating had always been the farthest thing from my mind. As a single mom who ran two businesses and rescued dogs in my free time, I never had the mental bandwidth to date. I concentrated on my kid and keeping a roof over his head. But now, except for my dogs, I was alone. Maybe it was time to put myself out there, but considering I knew most of the men my age in Heywood, the dating pool was pretty small. They were either married or just plain losers. I'd already gone the loser route, and I wouldn't do that again. And I certainly had no interest in becoming the other woman. That role hadn't played out too well for Phoebe.

I answered my work emails, made a note on my to-do list to pay the water bill, then turned to my writing. After glancing over my outline, I placed my hands on the keyboard and prayed for the words to flow freely.

An hour flew by, and I sat back in my chair and stared at the screen, very pleased with what I'd accomplished. Despite my worry about Vic, me missing my son and Daisy's soft snores, I'd done excellent work.

I stood and exited the bedroom to go

check on Vic. Sing raised his head as I peeked around the corner, but then laid it back down again. He still stood watch over my sleeping brother.

For a long moment, I stared at the big oaf—the human one, not the canine. He drove me absolutely crazy sometimes, but in the end, he was my big brother. When he found out my ex-husband had laid hands on me, Vic offered to kill him, and had meant it. After I mentioned that the deadbeat wasn't paying child support, he went around every so often and roughed him up. When I'd been accused of murdering the loser, Vic had volunteered to say he'd done it just so I could get out of jail. My brother had been there when it truly mattered. He had many, many flaws, but his heart was usually in the right place.

The phone buzzed in my pocket. I pulled it out and glanced at the screen. Our father. I quickly sent it to voicemail. Yes, I loved my dad, but I wasn't going to be the one to break the news that Vic was passed out on my couch and may be going to jail for murdering his ex-girlfriend. I'd only met Phoebe a couple of times, but she'd always been nice. I just really hoped she'd been kicked by a horse.

I returned to my bedroom and quietly shut the door. After taking my place at my computer again, I outlined the next chapter for the book I was ghostwriting and then did a little research. It was a love story based in the future on a spaceship, so I had a bit of leeway for creativity. However, I did have to be correct on things like gravity and engine propulsion. It was enough to make my eyes glaze over and start a headache in the back of my skull.

Suddenly, the quiet of the house seemed oppressive, and I was reminded of the emptiness. The person I loved the most was now gone.

Tears sprang into my eyes and I quickly swiped them away. I hated crying. I supposed that I was like my brother and father in that way. I wasn't good with feelings. It wasn't until I was well into my thirties that I realized our mother's departure had caused us to become a family of emotionally stunted people.

I checked the clock again. Time to head to the salon. Usually, I took the dogs in case they found someone they liked. Daisy had explained to me that it wasn't the human who picked the dog, but visa-versa. When the dog decided on their human, they did cute little things to let the person know they were a match. Maybe a longing stare with big eyes, a paw in the palm, or a loveable tail wag and a kiss. Frankly, after she'd enlightened me, I realized it was nothing but manipulation. I was impressed, especially since I'd spent decades thinking humans chose their canine companions.

Today, it seemed all my dogs were happy with their current situation. Sing with Vic, Banshee with the food bowl, and Daisy sacked out on the bed.

"Do you want to go to the nail salon with me?" I asked quietly, secretly hoping the dog would say yes.

"No," she whispered, her eyes still

closed. "Shh. I'm having good dreams. Bunnies. Open fields. I'm running sooo fast."

I chuckled and hurried into the kitchen to grab my bag. I left Vic a note and told him to lock up if he left. Then, I headed down to File It Away, where I was sure the gossip vine would be on complete fire with Phoebe's death, and hopefully, I'd find out what happened to the poor woman.

CHAPTER 4

I ARRIVED a few minutes before my first appointment. After turning on the lights, I got the air conditioner going and checked my supplies. When my first customer walked through the door, I was ready.

"Hey, Jillian!" I greeted her. The scrubs straining over her thick thighs and her brown hair worn high in a ponytail indicated she was either on her way to work at the emergency clinic or on her way home. "How's it going?"

"Good. I'm done for the day." She glanced around. "Where are the dogs?"

"They decided to stay home."

She furrowed her brow. "That's disappointing. It's one of the reasons I love coming here."

"I thought you liked my store because of my amazing skills and rainbow-like personality."

"Right," she snorted.

I smiled, trying to be offended, but frankly, I couldn't care less what people thought of me. "I've got you down for a pedicure today." Quickly, I studied her hands. "I know you don't want to do a full set of nails, but let's at least get those things buffed out, okay?"

She nodded and I motioned for her to sit down at one of the bowls. Jillian and I had grown up together, but we had never been really close. As a nurse, she had shared that nails were not her friend when working on patients, which I completely understood. People who went to the emergency clinic were pretty banged up to begin with. They didn't need their nurse scratching them up or a lost acrylic nail in an open wound.

"So what's new?" I asked while her feet soaked and I buffed out her fingernails.

"Not a lot," she sighed. "We delivered a healthy baby yesterday. Mom and son are doing great, and Dad didn't faint during the delivery, so that was nice."

"Excellent." Sure, I was happy for the woman and baby, but I was wondering if she'd heard anything about Phoebe's death. "Any other news? Any big car crashes? Tractor accidents? Anyone die?"

"Why in the world would you ask me if anyone has died?"

I shrugged. "Just curious."

"That's a weird thing to be curious about, Gina. Are you feeling okay?"

When the door chimes rang, it signaled my second appointment. I scheduled people close so I could pack as many in as possible. I had to move quickly and efficiently to keep everyone on time.

Adrienne, one of the owners from Never Quit Wining, our local wine shop, walked in and smiled. Tall and lanky with flaming red hair, she was one of those people who was stunningly beautiful but didn't realize it. I appreciated that about her. With a grin, I motioned her to take the chair next to Jillian. "What's shaking, Adrienne?" I turned on the water to her bowl, made sure it was warm but not too hot, then turned back to Jillian.

"Not a lot," she said. With a groan, she plopped down as if she were exhausted. "I heard today that Phoebe Williams died."

Now we were getting somewhere. "Oh, really?" I kept my gaze firmly fixed on Jillian's hand. "What happened? She seems awfully young to have just dropped over."

"She's about your age, Gina," Adrienne said innocently. "It could happen."

Jillian and I exchanged looks. With both of us approaching fifty, I supposed to someone like Adrienne—who was in her late twenties—we may appear ancient and ready to drop dead at any time. Goodness knew I sometimes felt like I could.

"Phoebe was young and fit," Jillian said. "There's no way she died suddenly unless she had some medical condition she wasn't aware of. My guess is she had an accident with one of the horses."

After shutting off the water at Adrienne's bowl, I motioned for her to place her feet in and began working on Jillian's toes as the two women continued to talk, but the conversation had moved on to Adrienne's store and how she and her husband, Wayne, grew their own grapes to make their organic wine. I half listened, still preoccupied with Phoebe's death. Thankfully, I had the list of suspects Vic and I had made at home to present to Mallory if she decided to gun for my brother.

Just as I was about done with Jillian and halfway through with Adrienne, the door chimes indicated someone had walked in. Glancing over at the door, I assumed the woman entering was my third client. Margaret, if I remembered correctly. When she made the appointment, she claimed she was new in town. I smiled and waved her over to the last seat, which also happened to be the bowl where I'd found my ex-husband murdered. He'd been drugged with horse tranquilizer then drowned in the foot bowl. That had been a bad day, which had led to me being jailed for his demise. It was my store and everyone knew I hated him, so I couldn't really blame the sheriff for thinking I did it.

"Hello," she said softly. I pegged her somewhere in her thirties and based on the muscular legs straining against the fabric of her slacks, maybe a long-distance runner. Or an avid biker. "I have an appointment. My name's Margaret."

"I'm Gina," I said, pleased I'd remembered her name correctly. "We talked on the phone. This is Adrienne, and that's Jillian."

The two women waved.

"Nice to meet you," Margaret said, taking her chair. "Thanks for getting me in today."

"Of course." I turned on her water and filled her bowl, then motioned to her to soak her feet. "So, tell us, Margaret. How did you come to move to our little slice of paradise in the Arizona mountains?"

"I ran the Sedona marathon last year, and once I saw Heywood, I knew we had to move."

"The Sedona marathon?" Jillian asked. "That's quite the run!"

"Thirty miles," Margaret said. "All the hotels in Sedona were full, so we ended up staying here at one of the Bed and Breakfasts. We fell in love with the area, so when the job at the police station opened up, I applied, and the rest is history."

The police station? Had I just found a new best friend? Certainly, working at the sheriff's office she'd have a lot of information to share.

I smiled warmly. "Welcome to town. We're glad to have you."

Jillian gave me a sideways glance as if I'd temporarily misplaced my brain. I wasn't usually that nice and sincere, especially to strangers.

"How do you like working for the sheriff?" Adrienne asked. Unlike me, I knew she had no other motive than to be friendly.

"Oh, it's a great job," Margaret enthused. "I'm really enjoying it. I'm surprised how busy it is for being such a small department, though." She glanced at the front door, then lowered her voice. "How many murders happen around here a year?"

"Why?" the three of us asked in unison.

"There was one last night," she said. "A woman who works at a horse farm."

I kept my gaze firmly focused on Adrienne's feet as she gasped. "Phoebe was murdered? Are you sure?"

Margaret nodded. "I read the report before I came in. At first, they thought maybe she'd been kicked by a horse, but the coroner says she was hit from behind by a long, round object."

The fact of the matter was that there seemed to be a lot of murders taking place in Heywood, especially since we were a small, mountain town that relied heavily on tourists. Sheriff Mallory had mucked up the investigation on all of them and my friend, Sam Jones, and been instrumental in solving them. But Sam was now traipsing around the world with her new-found millions of dollars and her boyfriend. Being a soap opera star paid well.

"I wonder what the round object could be," Adrienne mused. "And who would want Phoebe dead."

"Apparently she had an ex-boyfriend who was a bit sketchy," Margaret said. "The sheriff is trying to locate him."

I bit my lip to stifle my groan. Dang it. Odds were very good she was speaking of Vic.

"I'm heading out," Jillian said, handing me some bills. "I'll see you later, Gina. Thanks for my pretty toes."

"You're welcome," I called to her as she strolled out the door. "Have a good one!"

I turned my attention back to Adrienne's feet. "What else did the sheriff say about Phoebe's death?" I asked. "Anything interesting?"

"Well, I probably shouldn't be talking about an open investigation," Margaret sniffed. "It's still in the preliminary stages."

I smiled and nodded to hide my irritation. "Of course."

While I was thinking of other ways to pry the information out of Margaret, Adrienne chatted about wine and invited Margaret to her store for samples. "You can come too, Gina," she said. "We've got a new Merlot that's really good."

"Just let me know when to be there," I said. "I'd never pass on wine samples."

The door chimes indicated another customer. I glanced up to greet them, but my smile quickly faded.

Sheriff Mallory Richards strolled in. I whispered a curse as she grinned at me. I didn't have her on the schedule, so she didn't want her nails done. Considering we didn't like each other much and I'd just discovered Phoebe had been murdered, this wasn't a social visit.

"Ms. Dunner," she greeted me.

"Sheriff!" Margaret exclaimed. "What are you doing here?"

"Hello, Margaret. I'm here to speak to Ms. Dunner. I see you're getting a pedicure, despite the fact we have a murder to solve."

"Y-yes, ma'am," she stammered. "I'm on my lunch hour. Was I not supposed to take it?"

Mallory glared at her, then turned her gaze to me. "How's everything going today, Ms. Dunner?"

"Everything was going good... until now."

Margaret gasped while Adrienne's eyes widened. Mallory glared daggers at me. "What does that mean?" she asked. "You aren't happy to see me?"

I sighed and returned to my work—painting Adrienne's toenails purple. "Did you want to make an appointment?" I asked. "I'm full today but I can get you in on Friday."

"No." She strolled around the store, stopping at the rack that held hundreds and hundreds of bottles of toenail polish. She picked up a cherry red and rolled it around in her palm. "I'm wondering where your brother is."

"Haven't seen him," I lied. No way was I sending her to my house to fetch him.

"Are you sure about that?"

"Absolutely," I said. "When I left the ranch with him this morning, I dropped him off at my father's."

"Hmm, that's interesting. I was just at your father's house and he hasn't seen Vic. Do you think he's a liar, Gina? Or are you?"

Crud.

I glanced at Margaret as she stared at me, finally realizing that I was the accused's sister, and probably regretting she ever stepped foot in my shop. "I don't know where he is," I repeated.

"Then you won't mind if I stop by your place and take a look around," Mallory said.

"Actually, I do mind." I placed the brush back into the purple polish, set it on the floor and stood, crossing my arms over my chest. "I have rescue dogs at home, all who have suffered great trauma. Having strangers at the house upsets them, and I'm not letting you inside unless I'm there and you have a warrant."

She smiled as she continued to roll the bottle of nail polish in her palms. "I'm just going to knock on the door."

"Are you going to clean up the pee after they wet themselves from the fear of having a stranger at the front door?" I shot back. When she didn't answer, I said, "Stay away from my house unless I'm there."

I returned to my stool, took a deep breath, and continued to paint Adrienne's toenails. Purple was not the color I would've chosen for her. Would the dogs wet themselves? Probably not. They'd been with me long enough where they realized they were finally safe. I just didn't want Mallory near my house, especially with Vic passed out on the couch.

The chimes rang again, and I glanced up to see the sheriff had departed. I sighed with relief, then smiled at Margaret. "Your boss and I don't get along."

"I can see that."

One thing had just become very certain: I'd have to find Phoebe's killer because the sheriff was definitely gunning for my brother.

He may be a jerk at times, he may make bad decisions, but he wasn't a murderer.

I just had to prove it.

CHAPTER 5

HOURS LATER, I closed up shop and hurried home. Based on the groans coming from the living room as I walked through the front door, Vic had one heck of a hangover.

Daisy greeted me with a string of sentences I could barely decipher, she spoke so quickly. "Where have you been? Where have you been?" Daisy said. "I missed you sooo much! Where did you go? Why didn't you take me? Did I tell you I missed you?"

I glanced down at the little brown and white dog as her tail wagged so hard, I was afraid she was going to bust her spine. I bent over to pet her. "I'm glad to see you, too," I whispered. "I had to go to work so I have money to feed you. I asked you to go with me but you told me your dreams of bunnies and open fields were more important."

"Oh! I remember now!"

At the mention of food, Banshee barked from the kitchen. I found her just where I'd left her—sitting right next to the food bowl, her tail wagging as well.

I tapped Banshee's head, filled the bowls, poured a glass of water, then went to see Vic. I found him sitting up on the couch with his head in his hands, Sing still at his side.

"Why did you let me drink all that whisky this morning?" he asked.

I handed him the water and sat down in a chair. "Like I had any say."

He drank greedily, finishing it off, then set the glass on the coffee table. "Man, I feel awful."

"Well, I hate to make you feel worse,

but Phoebe was murdered and the sheriff really, really wants to talk with you."

He groaned and laid his head against the cushions. "I'm done for. She's going to take me down for it."

I shrugged. "Maybe, maybe not. We've got a good list of other suspects. Don't forget about that."

"You're right. I forgot we talked about it this morning."

"Whisky will do that to you."

"Gina! Gina! Gina!" Daisy screeched. "I have to go potty! Hurry! Oh, my gosh, hurry!"

I raced into the kitchen to find Banshee and Daisy both dancing by the back door. I opened it and they ran outside. I left the door wide so they could return at their leisure. Besides, there was a nice breeze and I hoped to cool the house without turning on the air conditioner.

Returning to the living room, I eyed Sing. "You should go out as well."

He didn't move, and I had no idea if he understood me. Daisy had once told me his family was Asian, so chances were good he couldn't. Or my conversations with Daisy were all in my head and no dog really understood a word I said, but I didn't like to think about that. However, my life would be much easier if I could chat with all dogs, not just Daisy.

"Quit talking to dogs," Vic groaned. "They can't understand a word you say, Gina."

I rolled my eyes as Sing laid his head on Vic's lap. Was he claiming Vic as his? He seemed pretty attached.

"You need to get out of here," I said. "Mallory is looking for you. She's already been to Dad's and she's talking about coming here."

Vic opened his eyes and sat up. "Really?"

I nodded.

"Where am I supposed to go?" he asked, spreading his arms wide. "I can't go to my place on the ranch. I'm probably not wanted there anyway. I can't go to Dad's. It's not like I can check into the bed and breakfast down the street, either. You can't kick me out, Gina."

"Well, if you do stay here, Mallory is going to come and haul you to jail."

"Now that I know she's looking for me, I won't be seen."

I had my doubts. Could I get in trouble for him being in my home? Aiding and abetting or some legalese garbage like that?

"I need to go," I said, standing.

"But you just got home."

"I know," I replied. "I've got things to do, people to see."

"Does that mean I can stay?" he asked.

I shrugged and sighed. "I guess so. I don't know where else to put you. Just don't get me in trouble and get caught being here, okay?"

"Where are you off to?"

"To get some advice on how to figure out who really killed Phoebe."

"Can I go? Can I go?" Daisy asked as she ran into the room. "Take me! Let's go!"

Although I would prefer to leave her at

home, I decided not to argue. She stood at the door, staring at it, as if she willed it to open. Besides, I needed to get the scoop on Sing. Why was he curling up with my brother? Was it a match, and if so, why had it taken so long? Sing had met my brother many times beforehand.

"Let me get a leash," I sighed. Once I had Daisy hitched up, I turned to Vic. "Don't answer the door. Pull the blinds, and if Mallory shows up with a warrant, run."

"Dad's calling… again," he said, picking up his buzzing phone from the coffee table. "I don't know what to tell him."

"Try the truth," I said. "He already knows something's wrong because Mallory was at his house asking where you were. Maybe he has some ideas on how to figure out who really killed Phoebe."

As I left the house, I scanned the street, half expecting to find a couple of sheriff's vehicles, but it was clear.

Daisy jumped into the car, and I slid behind the steering wheel.

"Can we go down to the Riverwalk?" Daisy asked.

"Not today," I replied. "I've got too much to do."

"But I love it there, Gina," she whined. I glanced in the rearview mirror to find her head down, but her gaze met mine. She was pouting.

"Sorry," I muttered. Her sulking usually got her what she wanted, but not today. "I have to go see Annabelle. Maybe Jack, Annabelle's dog, will be there. Now tell me what's going on with Sing. He hasn't left my brother's side since he arrived."

"I know. I asked him about it earlier, but he didn't say much. He just said he felt Vic needed to be aware someone was at his side."

"So Sing hasn't claimed Vic as his own?"

"Not that he's mentioned to me."

I would love it if Sing found a home, and now that I had given it some consideration, Vic wouldn't be a bad option. He lived out at Diamond Ranch and worked all day. Sing could either hang out on the couch or roam the grounds. Knowing Sing and his laziness, he'd prefer the couch.

Well, I should say they may be a good match if Vic wasn't in prison. Maybe the dog was waiting to claim him until he was sure my brother wouldn't be spending time in jail.

A few moments later, we pulled up in front of Sage Advice, the local herbal apothecary. I stared at the building for a long moment. My friend, Sam Jones, was the owner, and also the one I really wanted to talk to about how to solve Phoebe's murder because she'd been the one to find the real killers in the previous murders that had taken place in our small town. But since she was traveling, I decided to talk to her assistant, Annabelle. Both of us had helped Sam solve the murders, but Annabelle had been with her almost every step of the way since they worked together. I was hoping for some tips.

"Let's go," I said. We exited the car and Daisy ran ahead toward the door.

As I stepped inside, my heart ached. For some reason, I had hoped Sam would be standing behind the counter. I was having some feelings of abandonment with her and my son leaving in such a short period of time.

To my right stood floor to ceiling glass shelving holding labeled mason jars of herbs. Glass tables scattered the floor featuring the product Annabelle made, such as soaps and tinctures. The scent of mint and lavender greeted me along with Annabelle.

"Gina!" she yelled. "Oh, my gosh! Like, what are you doing here?!"

I did like Annabelle, but she was as quirky as they come. To me, she lived her life as if she'd never grown up. In other words, she was still stuck in the eighties. With crimped blonde hair, bangs standing almost vertical, heavy blue, sparkly eyeliner and her neon pink leggings with her off the shoulder white shirt that read

Simple Minds, she looked as if she was ready to go to a costume party. But that was Annabelle. She lived and breathed everything eighties and had no intention of ever updating. Not that I was a modern day fashionista, but I found Annabelle's vibe a bit weird.

"I wanted to talk to you."

She rounded the counter and took me into a tight embrace. Daisy ran through the store to the back room where Jack, Annabelle's beagle, usually could be found. Instead of insulting her choice in clothing, I said, "Nice leggings, by the way."

"Thank you! What's up?"

I stepped away from her as a headache began to form behind my eyes. Was it the neon or the stressful day I'd had? "Sam solved a lot of murders before she left," I ventured.

"Yes, she did. She's, like, so amazing."

I wouldn't argue that point. I missed my friend terribly and I hoped she'd return soon. "How did she do it?"

Annabelle shrugged and said, "Well, she talked to people."

I'd hoped for a different answer. "No secret truth serum you guys whipped up with all the herbs? She just talked to people?"

Annabelle bit her lip and nodded. "That's it. She listened for clues. Why are you asking about that?"

I sighed and closed my eyes for a long moment. "My brother used to date Phoebe Williams, and now she's dead."

Annabelle gasped and brought her hand to her mouth. "When did she die?"

"At some point last night," I said, even though it felt like I'd been awake for weeks. "Vic was the last one to see her alive, and you know how Mallory is."

"Ugh. Do I ever." She shook her head. "Do you know who else could've wanted Phoebe dead?"

"Vic and I made a list."

"Okay, that's a good place to start, Gina. Now you have to, like, go and talk to every single one of them and ask about their relationship with Phoebe."

And that's where the problem lay. Sam was likable and held her tongue when necessary. My filter didn't work so well, and I oftentimes said things I really shouldn't. This issue had gotten me in trouble more than once. Like the time Sam and I had been at a dance class and I thought I was doing a woman a favor by mentioning her flesh-colored leggings looked like she wasn't wearing any pants. We were asked never to come back. Or the time I'd mentioned to Jillian that delivering babies wasn't any different than delivering puppies. Or just about anytime I talked to the sheriff, which thankfully, wasn't often. I couldn't cut the sarcasm. I wasn't really a people person, especially around those who didn't appreciate honesty and a bit of snark.

"You know, she did have help from Jordan as well," Annabelle said. "You should cozy up to a deputy so he can feed you information on the case."

Ah, yes. Jordan Branson, Sam's boyfriend and now ex-deputy. Because why continue to work when your girlfriend was worth millions?

"Who?" I asked. "I can't think of one person on that force who I'd want to have coffee with, let alone cozy up to, as you said."

She pursed her lips together and stared off to her left. After a moment, she said, "What about Trevor Hutchinson? He's cute."

I was about to argue, but then I realized she was right. He *was* cute. Tall and blond with a piercing green gaze, but I didn't have any interest in dating him. "No."

"You aren't marrying the guy," Annabelle reminded me. "You're simply doing a little flirting in the hopes of getting information to clear your brother."

Okay, another valid point. As I considered hitting on Trevor, Daisy came running from the back room with Jack trailing behind her.

"Look, let me know if you need any help, okay?" Annabelle said. "But Doug is upstairs waiting for me. He's got dinner ready and it's late."

Doug, her boyfriend, was scoring points in the domestic department. I glanced outside and realized the sun had set. This day had been the longest one of my life and Annabelle was cueing me to get out of her hair.

"Thanks for the talk," I said. "Have a good night."

Daisy ran ahead of me as I walked to the car. When I slid in, exhaustion overcame me. The bone-weary fatigue was so great, I wondered if I'd make it home.

"Bark if I start to go to sleep," I muttered to the dog.

"Okay, Gina." She came forward from the back seat and placed her paws on the middle console. "I'll let you know if you're going to crash. But please don't."

After taking a deep breath, I put the car into gear and headed home. When tears pricked my eyes, I realized I was about to have an emotional breakdown. I swiped at my cheeks as they began to fall.

"What's wrong?" Daisy asked.

"I… I don't know."

But I really did. My son had left. Sam had left. And if I didn't find out who killed Phoebe, my brother would be gone as well.

I hated pity parties, but I couldn't help but feel everyone I loved was leaving me.

CHAPTER 6

THE NEXT DAY, I woke with the sun... and the stupid birds. They sang and called to each other, which was fine. I just didn't understand why they had to do it so early.

Daisy snored softly beside me on the bed. I glanced down at the dog beds to find them empty. Where in the world had Banshee and Sing gone?

As I rolled over, Daisy groaned, "Why are those birds so excited this early in the morning?"

"Good question," I muttered, sliding from the bed. After I placed my hair in a ponytail and slipped on my shorts and t-shirt, I didn't bother trying to coax her out of the bed. I knew from experience she hated mornings and would rise when she was good and ready.

"Can you shoot them or something?" Daisy mumbled.

With a snicker, I walked down the hall and smelled coffee brewing. For a second, my heart thudded with excitement because Jacob used to start the coffee pot and my mind played tricks on me, thinking he was home. Disappointment washed through me when I realized it wasn't the case, but instead Vic stood in the kitchen watching Sing and Banshee eat.

"Good morning," he grumbled, then sipped from his mug.

"Morning."

I pulled a coffee mug from the cupboard and poured myself a cup. After blowing on the liquid for a moment, I took a sip and almost spit it out. With a curse, I turned to my brother. "This is just one step away from tar. What the heck, Vic?"

"I like my coffee strong." He chuckled. "Pour some milk into it and it'll be fine."

Once I finally downgraded the coffee to something drinkable, I sat down at the kitchen table and began planning my day. I needed to talk to people, and a lot of those were at Diamond Ranch. But what business did I have at the ranch? None. I had absolutely no reason to be there.

"I need some clothes," Vic said, sniffing his armpit. "I'm a bit ripe."

A slow smile crossed my face. That was it. No one knew where Vic was. I could pretend I didn't, either, and visit the ranch under the guise that I was trying to find him so he could turn himself in. My stomach fluttered with excitement. It was a perfect plan, and if I could manage it, maybe I could get him some clothes out of his living space there.

After I explained my idea, he nodded. "Do you think someone is just going to confess? Because I can tell you right now, you're dumber than you look if you believe that."

I rolled my eyes. "I'll never look as dumb as you, Vic, and no, I don't think anyone is going to confess. But maybe, just maybe, I can get a clue or two so I can get you out of my hair."

We grinned at each other and drank our coffee. I realized I should also take Daisy. No one would appreciate a loose dog running around the farm, but she may be helpful in picking up scents that she'd smelled around Phoebe's body and identifying who had been around the poor woman before she died. Daisy had made it clear she'd detected other people—she just couldn't recognize them.

I finished my coffee and set my cup in the sink. "I'm going now, and I'm taking Daisy. Can you watch the other two?"

"Sure," he said. "I kind of like Sing. I've never paid much attention to him before, but he seems like a good guy."

I nodded and glanced over at the furry face. "Maybe if we can get you out of this, you should take him home. I won't even charge you an adoption fee." I didn't give him the chance to argue. Instead, I yelled for Daisy as I hurried to the front door. Hopefully, I'd planted the seed and it would flourish.

Daisy trotted down the hallway. "Gina, I haven't eaten yet."

"Let's go," I said. "You can eat when you get home."

"Quit talking to the dog!" Vic yelled from the other room.

After stepping outside, I glanced around searching for the sheriff's cars and didn't see any. They weren't getting ready to invade my home. If they did so when I wasn't there and they found Vic, I'd say that he broke in. I wasn't going to jail for my brother.

Daisy hopped into the back seat and I slid into the front. Once we'd backed out of the driveway, Daisy asked, "Where are we going?"

"To Diamond Ranch," I replied. "I have an important assignment for you."

"Yay!" Her tail wagged furiously. "I love doing important things!"

As I turned onto Comfort Road, I asked, "Don't you want to know what I'd like you to do?"

"Oh, yes. That may be helpful."

"When you busted out of the car and were sniffing around Phoebe, you said there were other scents there, but you didn't know who they belonged to, right?"

"Yuppers!"

"Do you remember them? If you smelled one of them again, would you re-call it?"

"I don't see why not."

"Okay. Your job is to run around and see if you can match up people with the smells from before."

"I can do that. What are you going to do?"

"Apparently, I have to talk to people to figure out who killed Phoebe."

Daisy snickered as she met my gaze in the mirror. "Don't offend anyone."

"I'll try."

We drove down the long, tree-lined driveway and my heart thundered. Why was I so nervous? Was it because I was lying about my reasons to be here? That had to be it.

I pulled up to the side of the big house, hoping no one would notice my car. Then I rolled down the windows in the back. After glancing around to make sure we weren't being watched, I turned to Daisy. "Go now, and try not to get in trouble."

"Yes, ma'am!" She flew through the window with ease and took off toward the back of the property.

That's where I would start as well. I grabbed my bag and slid from the car, then hurried after her.

I didn't see anyone while I made my way to where Vic lived. Six little dark brown houses stood side-by-side, and I had to admit, they were cute with their porches and flowerboxes. I walked up the two steps leading to Vic's and glanced around. I didn't see Daisy, nor did I hear any barking, so I had to assume she was safe.

With a deep breath, I tried to open

Vic's door. Locked. Good thing the big oaf kept a spare key under one of his empty flowerpots. I'd discovered that one night after bailing him out of jail and driving him home. A barfight, if I remembered correctly.

I slid the key in and hurried inside. All the blinds were drawn, so it took a moment for my eyes to adjust to the darkness. When I could see, I studied the small space.

Maybe five hundred square feet, there was a bed, a kitchenette, and a black leather couch. A television had been mounted to the wall. I was always surprised by how tidy Vic kept his living space. Clean dishes sat in the drying rack, clothes hung in the closet and the bed had been made. "He's neater than I am," I whispered, thinking of my unmade bed and the sink full of dishes. Maybe he'd become bored and clean up my house while he hid from the police.

I wasn't sure what I expected to find as I carefully made my way through the chest of drawers by the bed, as well as the bed-stands. However, a love letter to Phoebe wasn't it. I hated prying into his personal life, but I couldn't set it down. It was a side of my brother I'd never seen.

PHOEBE,

I'm sorry for the pain I caused you. I love you, and I

hate seeing you hurt, especially when I'm the reason for it.

I'll do better in the future. I know I'm my own worst

enemy. You are everything to me... the sun, the

moon and the stars. My life is brighter with you in it,

and I can't imagine a world without you. I know I sound

like a corny Hallmark card, but I don't know how else

to tell you how I feel. Please forgive me.

Please believe in me again. I want to be a better person,

and with you, I am. I want

IT ENDED THERE. And it certainly didn't sound like the writings of a killer. Or maybe it did? Maybe Phoebe had told him they'd never get back together and he'd murdered her? I couldn't really picture Vic going with the *if I can't have her, no one can* theme, but then again, stranger things had happened. I could talk to a dog, for goodness' sake.

I'd have to believe his story and in his innocence, until he was proven guilty.

After picking up a duffel bag from the floor of the small closet, I threw some of his clothes into it, hoping I'd made good wardrobe choices for someone on the lam.

Just as I was about to leave, something somewhat shiny in the corner of the closet caught my eye. I reached over and moved aside a couple of shirts, a pair of cowboy boots and a suitcase, then sunk to my knees.

"Oh, no," I whispered, reaching for the

metal object. About three feet long and circular in shape, it reminded me of the metal fencing seen throughout the ranch. Rust colored stains covered it. Blood.

Had I just found the murder weapon? And if so, what was it doing in my brother's house? Did this prove he'd been lying to me? Or was someone trying to frame him?

Without fully considering the consequences of my actions, I grabbed the pipe and shoved it into the duffel bag. My heart thundered as I set things back the way I found them. I then stood and hurried for the front door. I should've glanced out the window to be certain I wouldn't be spotted, but I'd been too rattled by my discovery. After locking the door, I turned around and came face to face with a man wearing jeans, a black t-shirt and cowboy boots. A little older than me with a mess of salt and pepper hair, he only stared.

"Can I help you?" he asked at last.

"Nope. I'm good, but thanks."

I tried to brush past him, but he moved back into my path.

"Who are you and what are you doing in Vic's house?"

"I'm his sister," I said, thrilled I'd come up with a great lie before I arrived. "I'm trying to find him."

"You don't know where he is?" the man asked. "The police are looking for him."

"Exactly. He should turn himself in and let court systems prove his innocence. I'm trying to locate him and convince him to do just that." Instead of being on the receiving end of his questions, I decided to flip the script. "Who are you? Do you know where he is?"

"My name's Chase, and no, I haven't seen Vic."

Wait a minute. Chase. He was on my list of people I was supposed to question about the murder! But why? That's right. He'd been passed over for a promotion. Vic thought it was because Phoebe was sleeping with the ranch owner, Roger.

"It's really awful about Phoebe, isn't it?" I ventured.

He nodded, his mouth set in a fine, grim line. "Yes, it is. I had to take over her job for her. We're all shook up, but pitching in where we can."

How convenient. He had the job he'd originally wanted now that Phoebe was dead. "That's really nice of you to take over her work. I hope they're paying you well for it."

Finally, he cracked a smile. "They are."

I'd been carrying the duffel bag over my shoulder with it behind my back, hoping no one would notice it. "What's in the bag?" he asked.

Crud. "Well, with my brother missing and the police wanting him for Phoebe's murder, I thought I better come here and get some personal items, just in case he goes to prison. Things I know he'd want saved."

"So you think he did it?" Chase asked.

I shrugged. "The fact that he used to

date her and he's now missing, it does look suspicious."

"Yeah, I agree. The cops were here looking through his stuff last night, hoping to find some clue as to where he might have gone."

"Did they find anything?" I asked.

"Not that I saw."

Based on the fact that I knew Phoebe had been hit in the head with a round object and I had a bloody one in the duffel bag, it led me to question whether the police were really that bad at their jobs, or if someone had hidden the weapon in Vic's house after the search.

CHAPTER 7

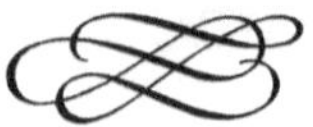

"I better get going," I said. "It was nice to meet you, Chase. Glad you finally got that promotion now that Phoebe's dead."

Confusion flickered across his face. "What?"

There I went again, running my mouth when I shouldn't. "Sorry. I'm glad you got the promotion."

I didn't wait to continue the conversation. Instead, I turned and hurried toward my car.

"Hey!" Chase called. "Why would you say that? I didn't kill Phoebe for a promotion!"

"I never said you did," I lied.

Just as I reached the car, I heard someone yelling behind me. "Gina! Gina! Hellllppp! Gina!" I turned to find Daisy running full tilt toward me, right by Chase... being pursued by a goat. "Open the door! It wants to kill me!"

"Oh, my word," I whispered. I flung open the car door and Daisy flew through the air and crashed into the back seat. I slammed it shut, then ran to the other side of the car. Just before impact, the goat came to a screeching halt, bleated at Daisy, who stared at it out the window, then trotted off.

"I'm faster than you, loser!" she called through the closed window.

With a sigh, I entered the car and started the engine before Chase decided he wanted to continue our conversation. I glanced over to find him staring at me, his arms crossed over his chest. It wasn't a friendly glare.

"Goats are scary," Daisy panted.

"Did you find anything?" I asked. "Besides the fact you don't like goats?"

"I smelled the same person in a barn that I smelled by Phoebe," Daisy replied.

This was good news. "Do you know who it is?"

"No. The barn was empty, except for the stupid goat."

I swore in frustration as I considered what the duffel bag held. I had a bone to pick with my brother. Was he the guy in love with Phoebe as the letter had indicated, or the killer as the bloody pipe suggested?

But when I pulled onto my street and noted two sheriff's cars in front of my house, I realized I'd have to deal with the cops first.

I almost grabbed the duffel bag but remembered what it contained besides clothes that were for my brother who I had sworn wasn't in my house. Then I noticed the front door to my home was wide open and my hands clenched in rage. What about my dogs?! How dare they!

I marched inside where I found Deputy

Trevor Hutchinson and Sheriff Mallory Richards looking around my living room. Vic was nowhere to be seen, and I wasn't sure if that was a good thing or a bad thing. Daisy followed me in and began barking and growling at the intruders, which loosely translated to something like, "I'll bite your face off, but if you get too close, I'll run so fast you won't be able to catch me." Yes, her bark was much worse than her bite. The sweet thing didn't have a mean bone in her body.

"What's going on?" I asked, ignoring her. "You better have a warrant."

"Of course we do," Mallory replied. "I don't want to have to shoot your dog, so go lock it up, please."

"Shoot my dog?!" I yelled. That escalated quickly. I turned to Daisy. "Quiet! Go into the bedroom unless you want to get shot!"

She growled one last time, then trotted down the hall. "Let me know if you want me to bite her ankles, Gina!" she called.

Trevor smiled as if he were really, really sorry for being in my home. Mallory handed me a piece of paper, which I couldn't read because my fury blurred the words. Or maybe I needed a new prescription for my glasses. I assumed I held the warrant.

"Where are the rest of my dogs?!" I shouted.

"Relax," Mallory chided. "They're outside. I do have to say, getting that little white one away from the food bowl was difficult."

I cursed again as I hurried to the back door to make sure they were okay. Banshee stared up at me and whined while Sing sat by the side of the house as if he were on guard, but I wasn't sure what he was protecting. Maybe he just liked the shade with the summer heat ramping up.

"Where's your brother?" Mallory asked from the archway to the kitchen.

"I don't know," I spat, turning to her. "Just like I told you last time you asked: I. Don't. Know."

"He's not here," Trevor called from the

living room. "Let's go, Sheriff."

She narrowed her gaze on me and crossed her arms over her chest. "I think you know exactly where he's hiding out."

"Even if I did, I wouldn't tell you," I whispered.

"I should take you down to the station," Mallory said, shaking her head. "You've got quite the mouth on you. Disrespect will get you tossed into jail."

Just as I was about to tell her exactly where she could stuff my disrespect, Trevor entered the kitchen and gave me another grin. "Sheriff, we've looked everywhere and Vic isn't here. Let's leave Gina alone, okay? Coming home and finding us in her house has to be pretty upsetting."

I wouldn't give her or Trevor the satisfaction of knowing that I was so upset, my hands were shaking.

"Especially since I asked you not to come in unless I was home," I shot back.

Where was my brother? Was he still here or had he bailed, leaving me literally holding the bag with the bloody pipe in it?

"Very well," she sniffed. "We'll be in touch, Gina. And, you do have a legal obligation to give us a call if your brother turns up."

"When pelicans fly out of your butt," I muttered as they headed out. After shutting the door behind them, I hurried through the house. Some things were out of place but overall, the police had been kind in their search. I checked every closet and even under the beds, although Vic would never fit there. Daisy sniffed around the house. "They were in every room, Gina!" she called. "Everywhere!"

I figured as much. My skin crawled at the invasion of my space and I glanced out the front. Both sheriff's cars were gone.

Where in the world was my brother?

"Vic?" I called as I returned to the kitchen.

No answer.

I glanced outside again and opened the back door. Banshee came running in, but Sing didn't move.

Then it hit me.

He was standing at the well that led under the house. I rushed over and jumped inside, then dropped to my hands and knees. "Vic?" I called.

"Yeah! Gina?"

"Yes," I sighed. "The cops are gone. You can come out."

I crawled out of the well and gave Sing a tap on the head. "You're a good boy," I whispered. "Thanks for keeping an eye on him."

As Vic struggled to move his girth out of the small crawlspace, I returned inside and sat down on the couch. Leaning my head back against the cushions, I tried to calm my anger, but said anger wasn't having it. Between me finding what looked like the murder weapon in his house, the police being in my home, and Vic hiding out from them, my nerves were frayed. And it wasn't even noon!

"This dog just saved my butt," Vic said as he strode into the living room brushing cobwebs and dust from his shirt.

I didn't even have the energy to send him back outside to finish the job.

"What happened?" I asked.

"He started barking and pulling on my shoelaces. When I looked outside, I ran for the back door and he stood at the front, growling. He must've kept them busy for long enough so I could slip under the house."

Sing? Growling? Huh. The chow didn't seem to have a mean bone in his body. Now I was surer than ever that he was claiming Vic as his own, which worried me. What if Vic had killed Phoebe? I couldn't have a dog attached to someone in prison.

"Did you go to the ranch?" Vic asked, taking a seat. Sing curled at his side.

"Yes."

"Were you able to get some clothes for me?"

I ground my jaw and nodded. "I also found something very interesting in your closet."

"What's that?" he asked.

"Let me go grab it."

Before going out to the car, I studied the street from the window. No cops for as far as I could see.

I hurried outside, opened the car door and swung the duffel bag over my shoulder. Daisy watched me from the entry.

"For a second, I thought you were going to leave without me!" she howled. "Don't leave me, Gina!"

She laid guilt on thicker than a Catholic priest. Not that I knew much about that, but I'd heard stories from those who had experienced it.

After taking a deep breath, I shut the front door and pursed my lips for a moment. I had to hold it together to get through this conversation with Vic.

"Gina!" Daisy yelled. "Gina! G—"

I sighed and scratched under her chin. "Look, I'm always going to come back to you, okay?"

"She can't understand you!" Vic yelled from the living room.

Daisy quirked her head to the side. "Little does the big dork know…"

I nodded and concentrated on the task in front of me.

"What did you find in my closet?" Vic asked. "If it's the Playboy Magazines, just know that—"

"Quiet," I ordered. I set the bag down and pulled out the metal piping. "This is what I found, Vic. And if I'm not mistaken, this is exactly what the coroner said Phoebe was hit with—a long, metal, circular… thingy."

The color drained from his face as his jaw slackened. "That's… that's not mine."

"Then why was it in your closet?"

"Uh oh," Daisy said. "Someone's in trouble, and this time, it's not a dog."

"I… I don't know, Gina."

As I stared at him, I was desperate to believe him. Yet, I still had doubts. Could he have killed Phoebe, even though he claimed he loved her and they'd been getting along? Maybe it had all been a lie to send me on a wild goose chase.

I set the pipe back into the bag, then plopped down into the side chair. "Look, Vic. When I was at the ranch, I met Chase. He said the police had done a search of your house last night. Either you did kill her and the cops are horrible at their jobs, which isn't that hard to believe considering their track record, or someone planted it after they left. I want to believe that you didn't do it, but I'm having a hard time."

"Why?"

I shrugged and shook my head. "Mainly because I can't believe the police force would be *so* incompetent that they'd miss the murder weapon in your closet, and you've had run-ins with the law more times than I can count."

He sighed and studied the carpet for a long while. Finally, he said, "I swear to you on our mother's life I didn't kill Phoebe, Gina. Someone is trying to set me up."

Considering we didn't know if our mother was alive or dead, I wasn't sure the oath meant much.

"What did Chase say?" Vic asked.

"Not much. Just that he was now promoted into Phoebe's position and he didn't kill her."

"That's convenient for him," Vic snorted. "He got what he wanted with Phoebe gone. I think he did it."

"I don't know," I said back and closed my eyes. "I'm not very good at this sleuthing stuff."

We sat in blessed silence for a long moment. Maybe even a couple. Perhaps I should consider leaving town and letting the chips fall where they may with Vic and his issues. But I couldn't trust the police.

I sat up and thought about what Annabelle had said. I needed a contact inside the police station so I'd have access to the information. Maybe Trevor was my guy. He had always been nice enough toward me, and as far as I knew, he wasn't seeing anyone. A little flirting wouldn't harm anything, and if I was lucky, he'd spill some secrets.

CHAPTER 8

BEFORE I GOT myself all dolled up to go cute-cop hunting, I needed to get some food. I hadn't had time to visit the grocery store in over a week, so the contents of my fridge were sparce. But the local restaurant, On the River, had some amazing breakfast burritos that were available all day long. I'd been in many times and picked up five or six of them, freezing them for future use. No one would think anything of me making a trip to the restaurant and taking home multiple burritos. Vic had to be hungry, and I was starving.

"I'll be back in a bit," I said. "I'm going to get food."

"Thank goodness," he muttered. "You don't have anything to eat. The only ones who have nourishment are the dogs."

"I know." I stood and grabbed my purse. "While I'm gone, please take a shower. You stink to high heaven."

"She's not wrong," Daisy agreed. "You smell worse than horse poo-poos."

I hid my smile and exited the house with a wave. I drove over to On the River and found my friend, Sally, manning the front door. She was also the owner and spent a lot of time in the kitchen. With her long brown hair, beak-like nose and wide eyes, she reminded me a bit of a bird. Maybe an ostrich or an emu.

"Hey, there, Gina!" she greeted me. Sally was a hugger and she grabbed me and squeezed. "How are things going?"

"Good," I grunted, then stepped away and cleared my throat. I appreciated the physical affection, but it still made me somewhat uncomfortable. The only one I ever felt truly contented embracing was my son. "I was wondering if I could scoop up a few burritos."

"Sure! Take a seat and let me get you a cup of coffee while I whip them up."

My mouth began to water as she led me over to a table by the large floor-to ceiling picture window overlooking the river and the forest beyond. She poured me a cup of coffee, and I quietly sat with my own thoughts as I watched the people strolling along the Riverwalk and the river rafters floating by. Despite the caffeine, my nerves calmed. The view always had that effect on me and it allowed me to study my problems—or I should say Vic's problems, that had become mine—with detachment.

What would be my next step?

My two-minute conversation with Chase had to be revisited. I had more questions for him about his promotion. But honestly, based on what Vic had shared with me, I really liked the theory of Roger becoming upset that Phoebe had broken off the relationship and killed her. That seemed more likely than her being murdered over a job advancement. But people had been killed for less. Just because I wouldn't kill someone over employment didn't mean someone else also wouldn't.

Sally slid into the booth across from me.

"Are you okay, Gina?"

No. Yes? Maybe. "Why do you ask?"

"I heard about Vic," she whispered, her gaze darting all around the restaurant. "I'm so sorry."

"He didn't do it," I muttered.

"I'm sure he didn't," Sally said. "He's been in here with Phoebe before, and I could tell she was the center of his universe."

Interesting. I couldn't imagine Vic anywhere but at the local dive bar, Hold Your Horses. "When was the last time you saw them together?"

She shrugged and shook her head. "I guess it was maybe two weeks ago? They were holding hands across the table, and he couldn't wipe the smile from his face if he tried."

"Did Phoebe look as interested in Vic as he did with her?"

Sally nodded. "They reminded me of a couple in love. In fact, after they left, I glanced out the front window and found them lip-locked. It wasn't a quick, friendly kiss, if you know what I mean. There was a lot of passion there."

As I sipped my coffee, I tried to decide if this was good for Vic's case or not. It could definitely point someone down the path of him killing her because he wanted her, but she was with someone else. Or, it could go the other way and prove he loved her and would never hurt her.

"Do you know Roger Wagner?" I asked. "The guy who owns Diamond Ranch?"

Sally nodded. "Yes. I've met him quite a few times. He and his wife come in often. He's as awful as they come, Gina."

"Why do you say that?" I asked, surprised by this news. Granted, I'd only met him a time or two, he never struck me as mean.

"I've overheard some of the ranch hands talking while eating here. He's cruel and violent. One guy claimed Roger swung a shovel at him for not getting the hay stacked fast enough. Another woman said he made unwanted sexual advances toward her."

So maybe killing Phoebe wasn't that big of a stretch for him, especially if he'd taken a swing at someone with a shovel. Hitting someone with a pipe wasn't much of a difference.

"He was having an affair with Phoebe and according to Vic, she was going to break it off," I whispered.

"That doesn't sound like something he'd approve of," Sally muttered. "You need to stay away from him, though. Okay? I don't want you to end up like Phoebe because you're going around trying to prove your brother didn't kill her."

"I don't have a choice, Sally. Trust me, I'd rather be doing anything else than trying to find the killer. But I can't let my brother go to jail for something he didn't do."

"You can hope Mallory will get it figured out right this time," Sally said.

I rolled my eyes as she chuckled, then glanced at the front door. She swore under her breath. "This woman is something else," she whispered. As she stood, smiled and waved hello, I followed her line of sight.

Roger Wagner's wife, Cynthia, was waiting to be seated.

As Sally led her over to a table, I tried to think of a way to begin a conversation with her. *Hope you got that wine out of your carpet* didn't seem appropriate.

Instead, I stood and walked over to her table, leaving my bag at mine so Sally would know I was still around waiting for my burritos. I slid into the booth across from Cynthia and smiled. Her blue gaze flickered as if she thought she might know me but wasn't sure from where. Thin with a chin length bob, she was most likely in her sixties. Spending time outside at the ranch had deeply lined her face.

"I heard about Phoebe, and I just wanted to offer my condolences," I said. "What a terrible tragedy."

"Yes. Yes, it was." Her brow furrowed. "Did you know her?"

"We were acquaintances," I replied. "But I know she loved the ranch and had recently been promoted, so I can't imagine the loss you must be feeling."

Cynthia tilted her head to the side. "Yes, she was quite the asset. She'll be missed." The tone of her voice indicated that Phoebe would not be missed in the least bit. "Do we know each other?"

"I heard that she was killed," I whispered, ignoring her question. "Who do you think did it?"

She stared at me a long moment before answering, then glanced around the restaurant once again. "The sheriff says it was an ex-boyfriend. They're looking for him now, and I hope they catch him soon. No one at the ranch feels very safe."

"You think he's taking out ranch workers, one by one?" That theory sounded like a terrible horror movie.

"We don't know what's happening," Cynthia replied. "We're keeping our eyes open and our doors locked, though. But I must say, I feel like I know you from somewhere."

I shrugged and said, "If you had to guess, who do you think did it? If it wasn't the ex-boyfriend?"

She sat back and laced her hands together. "I have no idea. Are you working for the paper?"

"No," I replied. I wouldn't be caught dead working for the *Heywood Sentinel*, mainly because their star reporter, Barry, was rude, arrogant and thought he was employed by the New York Times, not a little mountain town rag. "I'm just a very scared citizen. I know who you are, and I figured you'd have information since the tragedy took place on your ranch."

No need to tell her I was the sister of the man who everyone thought killed Phoebe and he was hiding out in my house.

"I understand that. Imagine living on the farm! My nerves are shot. I don't know how I'll ever get to sleep again until that man is behind bars."

Sally approached and smiled, setting a glass of red wine before Cynthia. Hopefully she wouldn't tie me with the beverage. After all, I'd ruined not only her dress, but her carpet, too.

But, what the heck? It was lunchtime! It must be nice not having to be productive for the rest of the day, or maybe she indulged frequently at noon and could still be beneficial on the farm despite the alcohol.

"What if… what if it wasn't him, though?" I asked. She took a sip and glared at me over the rim of her glass. "Just for the fun of it, let's say that guy didn't kill her. Who do you think would?"

Vic had told me Cynthia was aware of the affair between her husband and Phoebe. Not that I'd ever think Cynthia would admit to killing Phoebe, but I had to wonder if she'd throw her husband under the proverbial bus.

"If I had to guess… gosh, I don't know. Perhaps another woman? There were rumbles around the ranch that Vic—that's that man who the police think killed her—he was dating one of the trash hounds who hangs out at that bar, Hold Your Horses."

Trash hounds? I'd never heard that expression before. Not that I'd disagree with her assessment of the clientele, but I'd never heard anyone referred to as a 'trash hound,' especially a woman.

"Do you remember her name?" I asked.

"Debbie. Debbie Something. I know that's not much help."

Unfortunately, I knew exactly who she spoke of.

Sally approached the table again. "Cynthia, your husband called and said he was running a bit behind, but he'll be here in about five minutes."

I glanced up at Sally, who shot me a glare. She'd been listening as she hurried from the kitchen and back to her customers and I realized she was trying to warn me. Roger was on the way. Cynthia may not recognize me, but Roger would. "Thank you for your time," I said, standing. "I really appreciate it. It's so scary when something like this happens in our perfect little town."

Cynthia sipped her wine and smiled. "Of course, dear. What did you say your name was again?"

"Your burritos are ready," Sally interrupted. "Best to get them home before they go bad!" She grabbed my arm and steered me back toward my table.

Sally shoved the bag of burritos into my arms and piled my purse on top of them. "Roger just pulled in. Follow me through the kitchen so he doesn't see you questioning his wife about a murder that he's mean enough to commit."

If it wasn't Roger, I wouldn't put it past his wife. She'd said she thought another woman could've committed the crime. Maybe she'd been speaking about herself.

CHAPTER 9

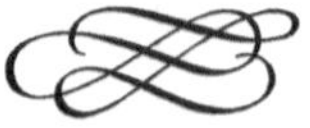

GROWING up without a mother had been difficult at best. My father, unsure of what to do with a girl, just raised me as a boy, which was fine with me because I had been a hardcore tomboy anyway. There were few rules and little discipline. I followed my brother everywhere—learned to ride bikes, make my own jumps and flew through the air with the best in town. I chased frogs, gutted fish, and learned to pee outside. During the winter, I raced down snowy hills on handmade sleds, built igloos and hid by the side of the road to throw snowballs at oncoming cars. My brother and I were children of the wild, even though we had warm beds to sleep in every night.

When I started school I realized I was different from most girls. My first inkling had been when I squatted behind a tree at the playground to pee and everyone laughed at me, especially the girls. After being reprimanded by the teachers, my father had been called. He'd listened intently with a furrowed brow as the principal berated me for not using a toilet and suggested I get some help with potty training. Then, he'd turned to me and said, "Sorry, Gina. You've got to learn to play by their rules now. Use the toilet, okay?"

And so began my indoctrination into a system I wasn't sure I wanted to be a part of. I longed to go back to being my brother's' sidekick and running wild.

I was in trouble more often than not. Apparently, hitting girls who teased me wasn't the right thing to do, and frankly, the tears my punches caused surprised me. It took me almost a year to eat with my mouth closed, and wearing the same filthy jeans each day was frowned upon by teachers and students alike. My brother laughed at all my mishaps, while my father apologized for not knowing how to raise a daughter.

Somewhere along the way, I was able to get my feet under me and became acceptable to society. I still longed to be the wild child I had been, but I also desperately wanted to fit in, so I did what I could in order to do so until I reached the age where I no longer cared what anyone thought of me.

Vic had other ideas. As he grew older, it became apparent he wasn't going to play by society's rules—only his own—and was always in trouble. Both of us loved and were drawn to animals. Vic found contentment working with horses while I tried to save every dog I could. He'd never admitted it to me, but if he was happiest while with the horses, it wouldn't have surprised me. I found my joy with my son and my dogs. I could really take or leave everyone else.

As I stared at Vic stuffing his face with his second burrito, I wondered if I should've gotten more than six of them. "Did you talk to Dad?" I asked.

He nodded. "I told him I'd be in touch when everything was smoothed over. I told him not to contact you or to come over here."

"That's smart," I said. "Did he ask where you were?"

"Yeah." Vic wiped his sleep across his mouth. "I told him the less he knew, the better it was for him."

Never in a million years would our father turn over one of us for a crime, whether we committed it or not. But, he could slip up and reveal something, so it was for the best that he remain in the dark.

"He sure is messy when he eats," Daisy said. She sat next to me, staring at Vic. "Which is good for me because I can clean up the floor."

I glanced over at Sing, who had curled up on the other side of Vic, and Banshee, who was in her usual place by the food bowl. All three watched my brother intently. I had a feeling Daisy was going to have competition in getting the fallen burrito bits. That was one of many things I loved about dogs—I never had to clean spilled food from the floor.

With a sigh, I stared out the open back door. Since Jacob had left, I'd been trying to find other activities to keep my mind occupied... like I didn't have enough on my plate. I'd found an old, wrought iron shelving unit and cleaned it up so I could grow some potted plants on it. The petunias and peonies were wilting, their green leaves turning brown. Watering them would help, but I kept forgetting to do so.

"I think I'll have another burrito," Vic said.

"Can you hold off?" I asked. "That's what's for dinner as well. I need to get to the store, but first I have to put some time in on my computer."

"I suppose so," he grumbled. "What about figuring out who killed Phoebe?"

"I need to keep the lights on, Vic," I replied. "I'm sorry you're in this position, but I'm doing the best I can to help you."

"We need to know what the police are doing to find the murderer… if anything."

"I think they've pretty much got you in their sights and they're simply arranging the evidence to nail you."

"But what evidence?" he asked, spreading his arms wide. "The fact she was my girlfriend?"

And your sketchy past.

"I'll be out in a while," I said, standing. "Then I'll figure out what my next step is going to be."

"I guess I'll watch some television."

Vic was usually busy, and I could tell the lack of work was wearing on his mood. The last thing I needed was for him to be depressed. I had to find things for him to do. "The closet door in Jacob's room is off the track," I said. "If you could fix that for me, that would be great."

I quickly rinsed my dish in the sink, wracking my brain for other things to keep him busy with. The problem was, he needed to stay inside. He couldn't be seen fixing my fence or repairing shingles on the roof. "And the knob keeps falling off the bathroom door in the hallway. You may want to look at the sink as well. There's been a slow leak for about a month now."

"Why do I feel like you're trying to keep me occupied with something besides my life going up in flames?" he asked.

I chuckled and turned to him. "The toolbox is out in the garage. I'm going to work."

As the dogs cleaned up the kitchen floor, I hurried down the hall to my bedroom. When my computer came to life, I checked my email to find correspondence from a potential new client looking for me to ghostwrite a murder mystery. A whodunit, as she called it, but one without gore.

I shook my head and typed out a reply,

but then thought better of it just before I hit send.

I was actively investigating to find out who killed Phoebe to save my brother from going to prison for a crime he didn't commit. I was in the middle of my own murder mystery.

"Gina?" Daisy called. "Can I come in?"

Before I could answer, she pushed the cracked door open with her nose and jumped on the bed. "Banshee's mean and wouldn't save any burrito for me," she pouted. "You have to get her adopted, though I'm not sure who'd want her. She's so selfish with the food."

And I had a talking dog. Maybe I could throw that into the murder mystery? The only problem was that I needed to actually *solve* the murder. I had my list of suspects, but no idea who had killed poor Phoebe. If Vic did go to prison, I could certainly make up the ending.

I jotted out a quick outline, then sent it over. It sounded a little nuts, but if she took it, I had another client. I went back to my romance novel set in space. I still didn't fully understand engine propulsion, but I was getting there.

"I think I should get extra treats today because Banshee didn't share the burrito with me," Daisy muttered. "It's not fair."

"Nothing in life is fair," I replied. "Now, please be quiet. I need to study."

A few moments later, I cursed when my phone rang. I was never going to get this book done. I glanced at the screen. Sally from On The River. "What's up?" I answered.

"Roger and Cynthia Wagner just left," she said. "They had a lot to say over lunch."

I sat back in my chair, my curiosity piqued. "I'm assuming they weren't discussing the horse farm."

"Nope. They were discussing Phoebe."

"What about her? Did they admit to killing her?"

"No. They're paying for her funeral, but they were really snippy with each other about it."

"Phoebe was sleeping with Roger, and Cynthia knew about it."

"You didn't tell me she was aware of his infidelity," Sally said. "It explains their behavior I saw this afternoon."

"What happened?"

"Cynthia had more than her usual two glasses of wine," Sally said. "She began talking louder, so I heard more than I usually do while running around. She was worried that people were talking and—"

"Did she specifically mention me?"

"No. Well, not that I heard anyway. She was saying that people were starting to gossip about the killing and she was concerned what it was going to do to their reputation, both personally and as a business."

"She doesn't sound very concerned about the woman dying on her property, just what people think of them."

"Exactly," Sally replied. "But anyway, they were discussing the funeral. Cynthia was telling Roger they needed to keep costs down. Called Phoebe a tramp. She kept getting louder by the minute, so people were starting to stare."

"What did Roger do?"

"I could tell he was very agitated. He asked her to lower her voice numerous times, but she just kept talking over him. Finally, he got up and left."

"How did Cynthia react to that?"

"Not much of a reaction, but she was pretty drunk by that time. Roger did say something before he left that struck me as a bit odd."

"What was that?"

"He said something about him hoping Cynthia was happy about the mess she'd caused, and he was angry he was the one who had to clean it up."

"I wonder what that meant," I mused. "It could mean that Cynthia killed Phoebe and Roger was trying to point the police in another direction." I recalled the bloody pipe I'd found in Vic's closet. Had that been Roger's work? Maybe when he realized that Mallory really liked Vic for the murder, he was helping things along? "Or, he could've killed Phoebe and he was trying to keep under the radar and Cynthia was there blabbing her drunk mouth."

"I didn't feel comfortable asking for clarification," Sally said. "I'm sure you can understand."

"Of course," I replied. "I appreciate the heads up on their conversation, though. If you hear anything else, will you give me a call?"

"Sure will, Gina. I know Vic didn't kill Phoebe. Let me know what I can do to help you prove it."

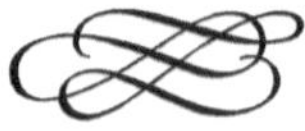

WHEN I'D IMAGINED APPROACHING Deputy Trevor Hutchinson and trying to charm him into sharing the police secrets about my brother's case, I'd have showered and brushed my teeth, then maybe found him in the coffee shop or suddenly bumped into him along the Riverwalk. I'd smile, maybe bat my eyelashes, and he'd fall under my wicked spell and tell me everything I wanted to know, and more. My plan hadn't included me in the produce aisle picking out some oranges only to have a couple dozen of them rolling off the display and onto the floor. I swore as I bent over to pick them up, and another one landed on my head.

"Ow!" I yelled as I sat down on the tile, surprised that an orange could hurt so badly. A baseball, sure, but an orange? It was way too early in the morning for this mess. If Vic hadn't eaten all the burritos the night before, I wouldn't have had to roll out of bed and hurry to the store. The man ate like my Hoover picked up dog hair.

"Let me help you."

I glanced up to find Trevor's lips trembling as he fought a smile. He stuck out his hand and I sighed. I hadn't showered that morning, I was covered in dog hair, and I'd forgotten to brush my teeth. Even though Trevor and I had known each other almost our full lives, this wasn't the best look for me, especially since I wanted to impress him.

"Thanks," I muttered. I placed my palm in his. As he yanked me to my feet, I sighed and pushed a lock of dirty hair out of my face.

"Looks like the oranges are angry at you today," he said. He squatted down and adjusted his gun belt, then began gathering the wayward fruit.

"Yes," I said, bending down next to him, but away from the stand. If they were going to continue to fall, I wasn't going to get pelted again.

"How are things otherwise?" he asked, not meeting my gaze.

"Fine." Even though this wasn't the way I'd planned to speak to Trevor about Vic's case, I figured I had nothing to lose. "How's the murder investigation going?"

He stood and carefully placed the oranges back onto the stand, one by one. "It's going."

I moved to the other side and began building my own pyramid of fruit. "Any new leads?"

He shook his head, then met my gaze. "Have you seen Vic around?"

"Nope." The lie came so easily. I didn't even blink.

"Do you know where he's gone?"

"Sorry, no."

We each grabbed more oranges from the floor and placed them back.

"It's important that we find him," Trevor said.

"Do you really think he did it?" I asked.

He reached down for the last orange and set it up on the pile. "Let's get out of here before these come toppling down again."

I nodded and grabbed my cart, then followed him to the cereal aisle. As long as we didn't touch anything, all the products should stay in place.

"Do I personally think he did it?" Trevor asked. "Probably not, but there's a lot of evidence against him. I'd like to talk to him so he can explain it all to me."

"Like what evidence?"

He smiled and tilted his head to the side, reminding me a bit of Brad Pitt. "It's an active investigation, Gina. I can't share that with you."

I narrowed my gaze. Maybe if I shared some information with him, he'd change his mind. But how much should I give?

"Well, I have some details you may find interesting," I said, glancing from one end of the aisle to the other.

His smiled faded. "Like what?"

"Did you know Roger was having an affair with Phoebe?"

Surprise flickered in his gaze for a moment, then he shook his head. "I didn't know that."

"And that his wife was aware of the affair?"

"Uh... no."

"Then maybe they should be investigated for Phoebe's murder," I shrugged. "Seems like both of them have more of a reason to kill her than a guy who was madly in love with her."

Trevor stared at me a long moment, then said, "Maybe you should ask Vic to come in and explain the fact that he texted Phoebe the night she died and told her they needed to get back together, and if she didn't agree, no one would be able to have her."

His words hit like a punch to the gut, but I remained upright and kept my facial expression neutral. What the heck was wrong with my brother? Why would he send a text like that? Maybe he'd been drunk? "I don't believe you."

"That's fine," Trevor replied, smirking. "I'm okay with that. It's part of the evidence. Can you ask him to come in and talk to me about it?"

Was he being sneaky with this ruse, or did he think I was just that dumb? "Well, Trevor," I drawled, my voice dripping with sarcasm, "if I knew where he was, I would gladly pass on the message. But as I've already stated, I have no idea where Vic has gone."

He pursed his lips together and crossed his arms over his big chest, mirroring my stance. By the second, I felt smaller and smaller as he stared me down. "Gina, I think you know exactly where he is."

With a snort, I shook my head. "I don't."

"Then why are you buying six pounds of ground beef, five chicken breasts and four steaks?" he asked, gesturing to my cart. "Not to mention the eight oranges. Based on your size, that would take you at least a month to eat all that, if not longer. But Vic? That may be a week's worth of groceries."

I should have considered my shopping cart before speaking to him. Of course, he was right. Being so busy, I didn't eat much, but an excuse came immediately to mind, and it wasn't that far from the truth. "I have dogs with special needs," I said. "Some need to be fattened up, others have digestion issues. This will all go to my dogs." There had been many times in the past when I'd been shopping for my rescues that my cart had looked similar. No dog would pass up a bit of ground beef, and dogs with digestive issues appreciated a little baked chicken.

Trevor arched an eyebrow. "It must be nice being one of your mutts."

"I'd like to think so." I sighed and stared at his shoes. So early in the morning and I was already exhausted. "Look, Trevor, here's the deal. I think you and I can help each other in finding Phoebe's killer."

"How's that?"

I tilted my head to stare up into those pretty green eyes. "We can pool what we both know and hopefully have it lead to finding who is really responsible for Phoebe's death. You already admitted you don't think Vic is, and I know he didn't do it. So, let's find out who did."

"Together?"

"Yes," I said. "Together."

A small smile tugged at his mouth. "I don't think the sheriff would appreciate that."

"I'm sure she wouldn't," I replied, shrugging. "But if we can solve the case, imagine the accolades you'll receive. Maybe you'll get your own parade."

"I hate that stuff," he sneered. "I like

being under the radar. And when has Heywood thrown a parade for a cop who solved a murder?"

Okay, so playing to his ego wasn't going to work because apparently, his was in check. "Never. But they should. It would be a nice community gathering."

He chuckled and shook his head. "Forget it."

"Well, if you aren't interested in accolades, then what about doing the right thing?" I asked.

Trevor had always been a good guy, but was he a hardcore rule follower? If he was, then I wasn't going to get anywhere with him. But sometimes, in order to do the right thing, rules needed to be bent or broken. Everyone knew that discussing active investigations with a citizen was a huge no-no for cops. And talking about it with the suspect's sister? That probably fell firmly close to illegal activities.

"You've got a deal," Trevor said. "But if at any time I decide that you're leading me down a bad path, or I find more evidence of Vic's guilt, we're done. Understand?"

I smiled and nodded. "Yes. This is going to be a great partnership, Trevor. But honestly, I still don't believe that Vic texted Phoebe the night she was killed."

He mumbled something about being a sucker for pretty women, then said, "I'll prove it to you. What's your phone number?"

I rattled off my digits as he typed them in his phone. With his pointer finger. Pursing my lips together, I hid my smile. I found it adorable.

When we'd finished, he asked, "So who else is on your radar?"

This was going so much better than I'd hoped. And I hadn't even needed to shower! "Besides Roger and Cynthia, I think Chase needs to be looked into a little more."

"Chase?"

"Yes. Chase Thomas. He works at the farm and was passed over for promotion.

Phoebe got it instead, and I understand he was pretty upset."

"Did she get the promotion because she was sleeping with Roger, or because she earned it?" Trevor asked.

"That I don't know. I've… I've heard from a good source that Chase told her to watch her back."

"We never considered him," Trevor muttered. "I'll have to pay him a visit. Who else?"

"Debbie Towerhall." Just saying her name left a bad taste in my mouth.

His brow furrowed. "Why her?"

"Vic was dating her and broke up with her to try to win Phoebe back."

"And where did you hear that?" Trevor asked.

"A source." If it wasn't obvious that I was in touch with Vic, Trevor was dumber than a box of rocks. "Look up her rap sheet, and you'll see why she needs to be questioned."

"I'm familiar with Debbie," Trevor said.

"I've been the arresting officer on more than one occasion."

We stared at each other for a long moment, then he nodded. "You've given me some good leads, Gina."

"You're welcome." A rush of relief passed through me. I had someone with skills and resources helping me to find Phoebe's killer.

"Tonight you and I should go to Hold Your Horses and see if we can track down Debbie," Trevor suggested. "That's her usual hangout."

I'd rather curl up with my dogs and watch a little television, but I also couldn't dump the full investigation on Trevor, especially if I wanted to keep an eye on who he looked into and steer him away from Vic. If that included going to a dive bar, then so be it. "Are you asking me out on a date?" I teased.

"Do you want it to be a date?"

Yes. No. Probably not. Maybe?

"I'll take your silence as a no," Trevor

said, bringing his hand to his chest. "Way to break my heart, though, Gina."

"I… I just… it's… I mean I—"

"Don't worry about it," he said. "I'll pick you up at nine."

Speechless, I watched him walk toward the cashier. If he didn't put my brother in jail for Phoebe's murder, I may consider dating him. But it had been so long. Did I really want to tangle myself up in a relationship?

"One step at a time," I muttered. I had to keep my eye on the ball—getting Vic in the clear.

But first, I had to ask my brother about the text he sent to Phoebe. Vic had never struck me as someone who would tell a woman that if he couldn't have her no one would, but again, I talked to a dog, so anything was possible.

CHAPTER 11

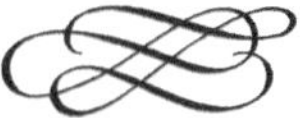

SINCE TREVOR WAS on his way to the checkout, I continued to meander around the store and keep an eye on him. I didn't want to give him the chance to back out, so I figured I'd keep my distance. When he left, I hurried to the checkout and paid, then rushed home to confront Vic about this supposed text he sent. I was back to wondering if he'd really killed Phoebe and was lying to me.

Daisy met me at the front door. "Gina! Gina! Gina! Oh, my gosh! I'm sooo glad you're home! Why did you leave me for so long?!"

"I didn't," I grumbled. "I was only gone forty-five minutes."

"It felt like forever!" she yelled, her tail smacking me in the leg as I tried to carry my bags to the kitchen. "I missed you, Gina! Please pet me!"

After setting my purchases on the counter, I leaned over and gave her head a scratch, then turned my attention to Banshee, who eyed me from next to the food bowl. "Hey, Banshee," I said. "How's everything going?"

"She likes having Vic here because he keeps feeding her," Daisy replied in an airy voice. "Pet me more! More love for me!"

I scratched behind her ears again and then yelled for Vic.

"In the living room," he called. "I can't get up, though. Sing's lying on me."

With a chuckle, I began putting away the groceries and my anger and stress dissipated. More than once I'd sat in the same position for hours because I had a dog camped out on my lap. After emptying my bags, I walked into the living room and took a deep breath, determined to have a conversation and not a screaming match, even though I felt like punching him right in the mouth.

I'd never seen Sing curled up near anyone, let alone plant two paws and his head across someone's legs. Yes—as I already suspected, he must be claiming Vic as his own. There was no other explanation for his behavior.

"I had an interesting chat with Deputy Hutchinson at the store," I said.

"What about?" Vic asked, stroking Sing's fluffy head.

"You." I took a seat on the couch opposite him. "He said they have a text message from Phoebe's phone from you that basically says if you couldn't have her, then no one would."

His brow furrowed in confusion for a second, then he burst out laughing. "You're pulling my leg."

"No. I'm not. This isn't funny, Vic. Did you send a text like that?"

"Of course not," he replied. "He's lying to you."

"I don't think he was." Placing my elbows on my knees, I massaged my temples, attempting to soothe the headache my brother had given me. It had never really left since he arrived.

"I'm going to say this once more, Gina. I didn't kill Phoebe. I loved her. I was trying really hard to clean up my act so she'd take me back." He pulled out his phone and threw it onto the cushion next to me. "Check it. I didn't send her that text."

"You could've deleted it," I muttered, meeting his gaze.

"Open my phone. Look at my texts. I've got stuff in there from three years ago. I don't delete stuff."

I picked up the device. "What's the passcode?"

He rattled off the numbers and I sat back against the cushion after inputting them. I went to the messages and scrolled through. There was a thread between him and Phoebe, but nothing about what Trevor had mentioned. Mainly a lot of work texts, but then one from a couple of weeks ago when they discussed getting a bite to eat. That must have been when Sally said they'd come in and were holding hands across the table, looking pretty lovey-dovey. The most recent text was Vic sending one red heart.

Then a sickly feeling hit me right in the gut. "Have you had this on?" I asked, quickly hitting the power button.

"No. I realized they may be tracing me."

Heywood was a small town and most police departments may have considered tracking his phone right away. Hopefully, Heywood's finest kept up their level of incompetence and hadn't thought of that step. Although, I felt kind of bad thinking of Trevor as a bumbling idiot deputy. But for my brother's sake—and mine—I hoped he was.

Just then, my phone buzzed. I pulled it out of my pocket as Vic said, "You need a shower. You're looking a little scruffy there."

"I know." The text was from Trevor. It was an actual screenshot from Phoebe's phone. Things like this could be manipulated, but I had a feeling it was legit.

I'M SERIOUS, Phoebe, it read. I need you back in my life.

You have to text me back. Please don't make me do

something I'll regret. If you won't be with me, you won't

be with anyone.

BILE ROSE in my throat and I turned the screen to Vic, my anger rising with each second. Why was he playing me like this? How dumb did my brother believe me to be?

He stared at the screen for a moment, his lips moving as he read the message. "That's not from me," he said.

Shooting to my feet, I dropped the phone on the couch. "Vic, that's a screenshot from Phoebe's phone that the police gathered! What do you mean it's not from you? What the heck is wrong with you? Why do you keep lying to me?"

"It's not from me!" he yelled.

So much for our civil conversation. "Yes, it is!"

"Stop yelling!" Daisy screamed. "Stop it, stop it, stop it!" She barked and growled, ran around in a circle, then placed herself between Vic and me, eyeing us both as she bared her teeth.

"Get your dog under control," Vic muttered. I noted Sing hadn't even raised his head from Vic's lap.

"It's okay, Daisy," I said. After I sat down, I clapped my hands and motioned to her to come to me. When she placed her head on my lap, I smiled. Dogs were the best companions and comforters. "I'm sorry we were yelling."

"I don't like it when humans scream at each other," she said. "It upsets me."

"I know it does. And I apologize." I stroked her head as I stared into her wide brown eyes. "Are you feeling better?"

"A little bit."

"You've always talked to the dogs, but why do I feel like you're having full on conversations with this one?" Vic asked.

I sighed, leaned my head back against the cushions and decided to ignore his question. "If you didn't send that text, then who did?"

"Who knows?" We sat in silence for a long moment. "Hand me your phone again."

I unlocked my phone, then gave it to him.

He studied the screen for a long time, then sprang up, sending Sing onto the floor with a yelp. Thankfully, the dog got his feet under and landed without issue. "Wait a minute! This isn't even from me, Gina!"

He handed it back to me, cursing. "Someone's trying to frame me."

I studied the screen, trying to locate what he noticed but I hadn't.

With his hands on his hips, he glared at me. "When was the last time I went by Victor?" he spat. "Maybe second grade?"

The message did indicate it was from Victor, my brother's given name. But Phoebe would have been the one to name the contact in her phone, and I was looking at a screenshot of hers.

"Never in a million years would Phoebe ever refer to me as Victor," he continued. "Never, Gina. She'd call me a dozen other things in her phone before she'd label my contact as Victor."

I met his gaze as he shook his head and his breath heaved. "Someone's setting me up, Gina."

Pursing my lips, I stared at the screen again. Between this and the possible murder weapon being found in his closet, I had to agree. Either that, or he was the killer and lying so hard, I almost believed him.

"Okay, Vic. I'll ask again: If you didn't send this, then who did?"

"I... I don't know. Obviously someone who hates me."

Unfortunately, that could be a lot of people.

As I considered the hard evidence against my brother, I realized if he hadn't committed the crime, someone close to both him and Phoebe had. Getting into Phoebe's phone and labeling a number "Victor"? And what about planting the murder weapon in his home?

"Gina, do you think Vic did it?" Daisy asked. "Because if you do, I'll bite him right in the—"

"No."

Vic glanced at me. "No? No what?"

"Just talking to myself," I said. "Vic, who had access to your house and to Phoebe's phone?"

"I have no idea. Everyone at the ranch knows where I keep my key. Some who don't live on property are aware it's under the flowerpot. Who had access to Phoebe's phone? Who knows."

"Did you?"

"No!" he shouted. "I didn't know how to get into her phone!" He paced the living room. "Gina, it feels like you don't believe me. That you think I killed her."

"All the evidence is pointing that way."

"But I didn't. You have to have some doubt or you would've called the police and turned me in by now."

He was right. Despite all of the proof in front of me, I still held on to a shred of hope that he was innocent.

"We need to figure out what number that's from," Vic said, pointing at my phone. "If we can get the phone number, then we can find out who sent the text. The cops can get phone records, right?"

I nodded and typed a text to Trevor.

V*ic* d*idn't* w*rite* t*hat.* Someone's *impersonating him.*

Find out the phone number of who sent that.

A moment later, my phone dinged.

THOUGHT YOU DIDN'T KNOW *where he was?*

I RESPONDED:

FIND *out the phone number of who sent that text. It*
may be the killer.

I GLANCED up at my brother. "You've got to give me something to work with here. Who do you think had access to her phone? Was she dating anyone else besides Roger?"

"Not that I was aware of," he muttered as he paced. Suddenly, he snapped his fingers and pointed at me. "You know, Chase worked really close with Phoebe. Some days, they'd be together for hours, going over inventory and working with the same horse. He could've easily watched her, gotten her passcode, and messed with her phone."

I nodded, wishing I'd had the where-withal to speak to Chase more when we'd previously met. Being caught in Vic's house had flustered me, though. I'd wanted to question him further before, but now, it was a necessity. The guy had a motive, the means, and the opportunity.

Roger and Cynthia were definitely good suspects, but Chase had just become much more interesting.

CHAPTER 12

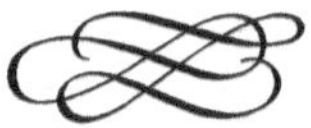

WHEN I CHECKED MY EMAIL, I was surprised to find the author who wanted a mystery written was on board with my story of an amateur sleuth with a talking dog. I wrote up the contract, sent it over, then went back to studying engine propulsion for my space romance.

"I can't wait to get this book done," I muttered.

"Me neither," Daisy sniffed from the bed behind me. "You're ignoring me and I don't like it."

Turning to her, I sighed. "I'm sorry. I've got a lot on my plate."

"When was the last time you took me for a walk, Gina?" she asked, her head tilted to the side while she lifted her ears. Her big brown eyes stared at me with harsh judgement.

"I… I don't know," I replied.

"Well, I do. It was four sleeps ago."

Yikes. It had been a while. Frankly, I was a little surprised she hadn't become destructive. Typically she had a lot of energy and usually began digging holes out back if she didn't get some exercise. "I'm sorry, Daisy. I'll take everyone for a walk later today, okay?"

She groaned and laid her head down on her paws. "I hate waiting."

"I know, I know." I turned back to my computer and for the next two hours, I wrote. The words flowed freely and when I finally sat back and crossed my arms over my chest, I smiled. The book was great and I was confident the author would like it—space romance, jet propulsion and the gravity of the dangerous plot included. Heck, I have even picked it up to read myself if I wasn't writing it.

"Here's a list of stuff I need to fix everything around here," Vic said from the doorway. I glanced over my shoulder to find him and Sing.

"Okay." I stood and stretched my hands over my head. He handed me the list and I looked it over. "I can get all this at Hammer and Nail Hardware, right?"

"Yes. I'd go myself, but there's that one small issue."

I chuckled and nodded. "Right. But just so we're clear, being wanted by the law isn't a small issue. I'll be back shortly."

"What about my walk?" Daisy whined.

"When I get back," I replied.

I glanced up at Vic to find him staring at me with a furrowed brow. "When you get back… what will happen?"

"Nothing." I glanced at my dog, her big brown eyes begging me to take her with me.

"Can I go, Gina? Please?"

Dogs weren't allowed in the hardware store.

"If you take me, I won't pee in the house," she ventured. "But if not, well, sometimes I can't control my bladder very well."

With a sigh, I shook my head. Blackmail at its best. "Fine. Let's go."

"Gina, who in the world are you talking to?" Vic asked. "I'm beginning to worry about you."

"I'm okay," I said as I hurried from the room, hoping to escape the conversation, with Daisy trailing behind me. After I grabbed my purse, I yelled, "Be home soon!"

As I drove to the hardware store, I made a mental note to check my text messages when I arrived. I was supposed to open the nail salon in two days, but last time I'd gone over appointments, I only had two customers. Hopefully, others had texted me to book. Otherwise, I'd be rescheduling the two I had. Or maybe I wouldn't. With only two appointments, it would be a short day, but perhaps I could get Banshee adopted. The more people she met, the better.

Daisy pushed her head out the open window, her tongue lolling out the side of her mouth while her ears flapped in the breeze. "Weee!" she yelled. "I love car rides!"

That was one thing I appreciated about dogs… one of many. The simplest things brought them so much joy. If only humans took note, me included.

I parked in front of Hammer and Nail Hardware and glanced over my texts. Make that three appointments for File It Away. I decided to keep my schedule, and I'd also bring the dogs. I wasn't one-hundred-percent sure about Sing claiming Vic —more like ninety-five—but if having him spend a couple hours at the nail salon found him a good home, that would be wonderful.

After grabbing my purse, I went to the trunk and picked up one of the leashes I kept on hand in there. After clipping it on to Daisy, I headed into the store.

"Gina, we don't allow dogs!" the cashier yelled. The young woman in her twenties named Erika, who also happened to be one of my clients, pointed at me with a long red fingernail that I'd put on her myself.

"I know," I said, approaching her. "I'm just going to be a minute and it's too hot to leave her in the car."

She flipped her black hair over her shoulder and sighed while furrowing her brows, which, in my opinion, resembled hairy caterpillars stuck on her forehead. I bit my tongue until it bled to keep from mentioning that to her. I meant no harm, I only wanted to help, but I'd also learned people didn't find such comments valuable in the least bit.

"Fine," she sighed. "Just make it quick. If my boss finds out I let you in with the dog, I'm going to be in trouble."

"You're the best, Erika," I said, smiling.

"Next time you come in I'll add some extra sparkles to your nails, free of charge."

She grinned, seemingly placated, but I didn't hang around for the conversation to continue.

"Gina, why does she have hairy worms above her eyes?"

I glanced down at my dog and snorted.

"Great minds think alike," I muttered. "We'll talk about it later."

My first stop was the pet aisle. I loved checking out the toys and treats and I almost always found something for the dogs. Today, Daisy gave a running commentary on every item I picked up.

"Does that have a squeaker?" she asked, eyeing the rubber chicken. "Banshee hates squeakers."

I set it back and picked up a rope toy. "Oh! Get that!" she demanded, her tail swishing back and forth. "I love ropes!"

"But I don't like it when you swallow them," I whispered. "It's kind of gross when I'm picking up your poops."

"At least I'm not a cat and puking up

hairballs," Daisy said indignantly as she sat down and glared up at me. "A little rope in my poo is not a big deal, Gina."

"Fine." I placed the rope toy, a rubber Kong, and a bag of bacon flavored goodies in my basket, then pulled out the list Vic had given me. As I rounded the corner, I bumped into Mike and Buck, the two biggest losers Heywood had ever known. With a groan, I rolled my eyes and didn't bother to hide my disgust. The two lived in the forest where they'd set down their mobile homes, drank beer, recycled the beer cans, shot guns and dealt drugs. Most in town considered them a menace to our quaint area.

They reminded me a bit of an ugly Laurel and Hardy. Buck stood tall and thin, but was missing most of his teeth. Mike was short and very round, and neither liked to shower.

"Gina!" Buck said. "What's a pretty little thing like you doing in a man's store?"

Mike laughed as he hitched up his

jeans. They'd never make it over his beer belly.

"Hoping not to run into losers," I retorted. "Now if you'll excuse me, I have more important things to do than waste my time speaking to you."

"You're a poet and you didn't even know it!" Daisy said, giggling at my feet.

"Listen, I was wondering where your brother was," Buck said. "You know, haven't seen him in a few days."

"I have no idea," I replied. "Gotta run!"

Mike grabbed my arm and yanked me so close, I could smell his body odor, a repugnant mixture of beer and unwashed man. "He owes us some money."

"That's not my problem," I said. Daisy growled at my feet. "And my dog doesn't like people touching me, so I suggest you let go."

He stared at me a long moment.

"Can I bite him, Gina?" Daisy asked. "Please let me! I've got a really good crotch shot."

"We've been to his house and he's not

around," Mike continued. "He needs to pay what he owes."

"Yeah," Buck chimed in. "We thought our warning would've made him pay, but it didn't work!"

"Shut up," Mike hissed.

"What warning?" I asked, now curious.

"That's none of your business," Mike said. "Tell your brother that we aren't playing any longer, and if he doesn't pay up, you'll be next."

"I'll be next for what?" I asked, now confused, but even more intrigued.

"Can I bite him, Gina?" Daisy growled again as I yanked my arm away from Mike's grasp and stepped away from him. The last thing I needed was him causing harm to my dog, or worse yet, suing me for a dog bite in his nether region.

"What's going to happen to me if Vic doesn't pay?" I prodded.

Mike and Buck exchanged looks, then Buck leaned in and said, "You won't like it one bit. Tell your brother to give us our money, Gina."

Goodness, did the man ever brush the remaining teeth he had? As they walked away, I tried to put together the pieces of their warning.

"Gina, I need to—"

"Shh," I said to Daisy. "Give me a second."

She sat at my feet. They'd given Vic a warning, one he didn't heed. The two had admitted to being at Vic's house. And, if he didn't pay, I wouldn't like what they had planned for me one bit.

What if they'd killed Phoebe as a warning to Vic to pay up? And then decided to set him up for it by planting the murder weapon in his house? Vic had said that a lot of people knew where he kept his spare key, and if he had dealings with Buck and Mike, maybe they were aware of it as well.

But what about the text message from Vic on Phoebe's phone? Were they smart enough to break into her phone and plant that?

"No, they're not," I mumbled. They

were so dumb, they were dangerous. However, what if they'd forced Phoebe to open her phone before they killed her? Maybe then they could figure out how to add a number and give it the name of Victor in Phoebe's contacts. Maybe.

"Gina, there's something—"

"I'm trying to think, Daisy. Please either hold it if you have to relieve yourself, or remember to tell me your thoughts later."

Okay, I could buy them planting the murder weapon. It's not like it was hidden somewhere clever. But setting up the phone? That may be a bit beyond their mental capacity.

"Gina!" Daisy yelled.

I glanced down at her, fully irritated. "What?!"

"I have something to tell you."

"Go ahead," I sighed.

"I told you I thought I smelled three people around Phoebe's body. Remember?"

"Of course."

"I smelled Vic, and then I smelled the skinny guy you were just talking to."

My heart thundered and I became dizzy. Suddenly, I felt as if I were underwater, the waves rushing over me. I needed to sit down, but instead, I grabbed a shelf. "You smelled Buck?"

"Is he the skinny guy?"

I nodded.

"Then that's who was next to Phoebe's body."

Holy cow. Had my dog just solved the murder? And if so, how in the world did I prove it?

CHAPTER 13

WHAT I COULDN'T DO WAS stand in the middle of the hardware store speaking to my dog about a murder.

That would get me a trip to the funny farm faster than I could blink. Instead, I brought my purchases to the counter, smiled, and nodded at Erika while she rattled on about her TikTok channel that I'd never seen. Something about a new dance craze and how many people had watched her version of it and commented on how beautiful she was. After I paid, I stepped outside. The rushing sound that seemed to encompass my whole body slowly faded.

I needed to ask Vic about Mike and Buck, but first, I needed to clear my head. After deciding to go see Annabelle at Sage Advice, I headed toward the store. Not that I thought I would actually get any sage advice, but sometimes a visit with my friend helped put my troubles away, or at least gave me a new perspective on them.

"What are we doing?" Daisy asked.

"We'll go see Jack and Annabelle."

"Don't forget Doug!" she yelped, springing from the pavement. "I like Doug!"

Doug had once been a homeless drug addict and had literally lived under the bridge down on the Riverwalk. This past winter he'd cleaned himself up, fell in love with Annabelle, and now helped her run Sage Advice. I'd never thought I'd see the day when Doug was clean and a functioning member of society, but I also never thought I'd have a talking dog, either.

When we entered Sage Advice, I heard Billy Idol playing from the back room. The store itself was empty. I knew from spending many hours with Annabelle that she'd be notified when someone had come in. I strode toward the cash register as she rounded the corner. When our gazes met, she squealed.

"Gina! Oh, my gosh. I'm, like, so happy to see you!" She took me in a tight embrace. "I was just thinking about you! This is kismet or something! Yay!"

I allowed the warm hug to penetrate my tired bones, despite the fact I wasn't a hugger and being held made me squirm. "I'm glad to see you too."

"Where's Jack?" Daisy asked, dancing at my feet. "Where is he?"

I released Annabelle and bent over to unhook the leash from Daisy. She took off into the back room searching for her canine friend. When I heard her bark, I knew she'd found success.

"What's going on?" Annabelle asked. I quickly studied her outfit before answering. A frilly black and white mini-skirt, black ankle boots and an off the shoulder white t-shirt. Large hoop earrings hung from her lobes, and bracelets danced up and down her arms. Her crimped, highly sprayed hair was held back in a black and white bandanna.

"I'm still trying to figure out who killed Phoebe," I sighed.

"Oh, no. I was hoping that whole mess would be done with. How's it going?"

"Well, I was just in Hammer and Nail Hardware and saw Buck and Mike."

She rolled her eyes and shook her head. We'd both lived in Heywood our whole lives, so no clarification was needed when I mentioned their names "What did those two jerks say?" she asked.

"I don't know if I'm reading too much into the conversation," I ventured. You know they're both dumb, so they may not have realized what they implied."

"Total mushy bananas for brains," she agreed. "Tell me what they told you and I'll let you know if your imagination is getting the best of you."

"Vic owes them money, and they've already sent him a warning. Now, if I don't pass along the message that they want their money and if Vic doesn't deliver it to them, they said I'd pay the price."

She arched an eyebrow, her mouth forming a perfect O. "Gina! They threatened you!"

Relief flooded through me. "You think so? Because that's what I thought, too."

"It also sounds like they might have killed Phoebe, if that was what they meant by previous warning…" she said.

Okay, so it wasn't me making wild assumptions about my conversation with them. Annabelle was getting the exact same vibe. "It was implied, right?" I asked. "That's what you think?"

"They didn't say it outright, but what other warning has Vic received?"

"None that I know of, but I plan to have a conversation with him about it."

She nodded. "To me, the first warning was them killing Phoebe. If they don't get their money, they're, like, coming for you next."

For the first time, a chill of fear traveled down my spine. I didn't scare easily, but I'd never been threatened with murder before, either. My fury immediately turned to anger. How dare they drag me into their beef with my brother?

"I don't like it when people mess with my friends," Annabelle grumbled.

She had a long history of exacting revenge on those who had wronged her and those she cared about. She'd stolen money from my ex-husband's house right after he'd died to make up for all the child support he'd never paid me. I sent my son to college with it. When the town doctor had messed with another one of our friends, she'd hidden a dead fish in his car. She'd broken into houses and placed plastic wrap around a man's toilet. She was the queen of revenge, and a small part of me longed to see if she'd give Buck and Mike a little taste of it for threatening me. On the other hand, the two could be very dangerous. Heck, they may be killers, and it wasn't that big of a stretch to imagine so.

"I can see the proverbial hamster on its

wheel while you're looking at me, Annabelle. I'll just say this: be careful with them."

"They don't scare me." She tilted her chin defiantly and crossed her arms over her chest.

"Who doesn't scare you, honey?" I glanced over her shoulder to see Doug walking in the back door from the deck. Tanned with a trimmed black beard, I noted he'd put on quite a bit of weight. He'd been skin and bones while addicted, so the extra pounds looked great on him.

"Some jerks who are threatening Gina." She wrapped her arms around his waist as he gently placed a palm on her shoulder and pulled her close. For a brief second, a shot of envy raced through me. I longed for that closeness with someone, to have another person to lean on, both emotionally and physically. Well, perhaps just a quick hug every now and then, not long, drawn out embraces. Maybe I was ready for a relationship.

"Who's threatening you?" Doug asked.

"Buck and Mike," I murmured.

Doug shook his head and sighed. "They're bad news, Gina. Steer clear."

"How do you know, Boo-Boo?" Annabelle asked. "Have you had dealings with them in your past?"

Oh, my word. She didn't just call Doug Boo-Boo. I pursed my lips to keep from laughing. Sure, maybe having someone at my side would be nice, but I would never in a million years call them some stupid pet name, nor would I put up with being called one.

"I used to get my drugs from them," Doug replied. No remorse. No embarrassment. Just a cold, hard fact. "They aren't very bright, and that's what makes them dangerous. Consequences don't seem to matter to them like they would to a normal person."

Perhaps I'd misunderstood the whole conversation with the two dolts. That could be a possibility. But the fact Annabelle received the same message as me after I explained the discussion made me quite uneasy.

Another bark sounded from the back room, then I heard the dogs running up and down the stairs.

"Is Catnip back there?" I asked. Sam Jones, who owned Sage Advice, was Catnip's owner. Annabelle watched him while Sam and her boyfriend traveled.

Annabelle nodded. "He'll make himself scarce once he realizes Daisy is here."

The cat and Jack got along fine, but Daisy hadn't had much interaction with cats. She wasn't sure whether she should fight them or try to make friends. Usually she ended up barking at the black and white feline with her tail tucked between her legs. Catnip had swatted at her a few times, so they were still trying to get their relationship figured out.

Speaking of volatile relationships...

"I guess I better go talk to Vic," I said.

This time, I hoped for more honesty and transparency than what he'd been giving me so far.

"Keep us posted on what's going on," Annabelle said. "Do you want me to whip up some tea for your nerves?"

"No, thanks." I'd tried Annabelle's concoctions before, and to me, they tasted awful. However, a lot of people enjoyed them and swore by their medicinal benefits. I simply couldn't get past the taste. "I'll let you know if I find out anything new, or if Buck and Mike come to slice my throat in the middle of the night."

"Oh, my gosh!" Annabelle yelled as I whistled for Daisy. "That's not funny!"

"You're right. Bad joke." I leaned over and clipped the leash to Daisy's collar. "I'll talk to you soon."

On the way home, Daisy gave me a running commentary on everything she'd sniffed while at Sage Advice and the conversation she'd had with Jack, Annabelle's beagle. I nodded and grunted every now and then, hoping to indicate I was listening to her. However, I didn't hear a word. I was too engrossed in my own thoughts.

While he was alive, my ex-husband had threatened to kill me a couple of times, but I always knew he'd never go through with it, even though he'd been physically abusive. There was a line even he wouldn't cross. However, having Buck and Mike indicate that they may just do exactly that had me a bit shaken.

Although I wanted to strangle Vic for putting me in this position of possibly having my life on the line, I decided I would remain calm and focused when I shared what had been said to me. When one of us became worked up, it didn't bode well for having a conversation. It usually dissolved into a shouting match and exchanging insults. We didn't have time for any of that. I'd wrap my hands around his throat later.

"And then there was a rattlesnake out on the back deck!" Daisy yelled.

That caught my attention. Annabelle and Doug had a quaint area at the rear of the store that overlooked the river. Tables and chairs had been set up, and they served afternoon tea and pastries. It was also a perfect place for a snake to make its way through.

"What?!" I shrieked, glancing in the rearview mirror.

Daisy giggled, the sounds reminding me of my son when he was a baby. "Just kidding. I knew you weren't paying any attention to me."

Cursing under my breath, I loosened my grip on the steering wheel. "You know those things can kill you, right?"

"Yes."

"If you ever see one, you need to get away from it right away!" I continued.

"I know. You've told me that. I *always* listen to *you*."

We pulled into the driveway, and I turned to face Daisy. "Don't joke about stuff like that."

"You weren't listening to me, so I had to get your attention," she said. After sitting down, she lifted her back leg and began scratching her ear.

"I know," I sighed. "I have a lot on my mind right now, though."

"Like how the skinny guy with most of his teeth missing is probably the killer?" she asked.

Right. Daisy had smelled Buck next to the body. I had no idea how to explain that, but I hoped Vic would.

"Let's go in," I said. "I can't tell Vic about you smelling Buck at the scene, but maybe he's got a reason for Buck being there."

"Or maybe I'm right and you should just listen to me. Buck is probably the killer."

But that was the problem. If Daisy was right, I had no way to prove it without mentioning to someone that I was chatting with my dog who'd happened to smell him by a dead body.

How in the world would I get evidence to nail Buck as the killer?

CHAPTER 14

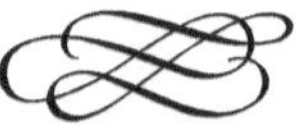

I STRODE up to my front door with Daisy on my heels. Sing began to bark, then Banshee joined in. As I opened the door, the two finally realized it was me, then quieted down, their tails swishing back and forth. After giving me a quick lick hello, Banshee hurried back to stand guard over the food bowls. How in the world would I get her adopted? I couldn't claim she loved to snuggle, and I doubted anyone would be looking for a mutt whose main focus was her next meal. Maybe in the right house where she was the only dog, she'd be able to get past her food obsession.

"Can we go on a walk now?" Daisy asked.

"Sorry, no," I whispered. "I have to talk to Vic."

"But Gina! You promised!"

"I know. My life's a little complicated right now, Daisy. Please have a little patience."

She glared at me, and I swore I saw harsh judgment in her stare.

"Did you get everything I needed?" Vic asked as he rounded the corner from the living room, interrupting our conversation.

"Yes." I handed him the bag. "But before you get back to work, you and I need to have a talk."

"I hate it when you say that," he sighed.

"I hate saying it." I pointed toward the living room and he turned around. We took our places on the couches and Sing jumped up and laid his head over Vic's legs again. I glanced down at my feet, expecting to find Daisy, but she was nowhere to be seen.

"What's up?" he asked.

"While I was at the hardware store, I ran into Buck and Mike."

Vic stared at me, expressionless. "And?" I'd expected more of a reaction, especially since he owed them money.

"They said that you've been warned, and that it's time to pay up. How much do you owe them, Vic?"

He groaned and leaned his head back against the cushions while stroking Sing. "Why in the heck are they talking to you about that?"

"They weren't just talking to me," I said. "They also threatened me."

His gaze narrowed. "Threatened you?"

"They said that you've been warned once before, and if you don't give them what you owe now, I would be the one to pay the price."

My phone buzzed in my pocket, but I ignored it.

He shook his head, his lips pursing into a fine line. "Those sons of—"

"What do you think the first warning

was?" I interrupted. Yes, I had my own idea, but I wanted to see if Vic would think the same.

"I don't know," he replied. "None."

Was he really this stupid, or was I reading too much into the conversation I'd had with the two dolts? And what about Annabelle? She'd received the same message as me. "Do you think that maybe Phoebe's death was the warning?" I ventured.

Vic's eyes widened and he swore under his breath.

"It makes sense, doesn't it?" I continued. "You owe them money and you haven't paid it back. They want to send a loud, clear message. The death of the woman you love is a pretty strong one, if you ask me."

He stared at the floor for a long while as he threaded his fingers through Sing's hair. "I can't believe they'd do that," he finally whispered.

"You said everyone knew where you kept your spare key, so I'm assuming they did as well. They could have planted the murder weapon."

"But what about the phone?" he asked. "How would they send that text?"

I shrugged. "If they killed Phoebe, they most likely had access to her phone. Didn't she carry it everywhere like a normal person?"

Having grown up in the era where the only phone available was attached to the wall, it still felt weird to think about always carrying around a device, but almost everyone did it.

"Yeah, she did."

"So what do you think?" I asked, once again ignoring my phone.

"I don't know if they're smart enough to pull all that off."

"I question it as well, Vic, but at the same time, we have to really consider them as the killers, who were delivering a message to you."

"But see, that's the thing," he said. "Buck was at the farm a day or two before Phoebe's death and I told them I needed more time to get the money together. They didn't seem to have a problem with it."

"Maybe they changed their minds."

"Maybe," he sighed.

Now to bring up the fact that Daisy had smelled Buck near the murder scene without actually mentioning it. "When you said Buck had visited, where did you guys meet?"

"Why?"

"I'm just wondering. Was it in the arena where Phoebe died? At your place? Somewhere else on the ranch?"

He stared at me as if I were ninety-nine cents short of a dollar bill, but finally he said, "I was working with a horse in the arena where Phoebe died. Buck and I talked there."

Dang it! Daisy could've smelled Buck's scent from that visit. Or could she? I didn't know how long an odor would last on the dirt. I'd have to ask her if it was possible.

"How much do you owe them?" I asked

again, fully aware he hadn't answered the first time.

"Two thousand."

I shook my head, not bothering to question him further. He'd either bought drugs or something else that may not be entirely legal. And possibly because of his bad decisions, a woman died. I didn't want to know the details of his purchase.

If my theory was correct on Phoebe being the first warning, I wasn't going to wait around to become the second. "I'm going to see Buck and Mike, and I'll pay off your debt," I said.

"Gina, you don't have to do that."

"Yes, I do," I grumbled. "My safety is my biggest concern right now. If I'm right, those two idiots are coming after me next, and I don't want to be looking over my shoulder."

When the doorbell rang, we exchanged glances while the dogs barked.

"Are you expecting anyone?" he asked.

I shook my head and hurried over to the window. We'd drawn the blinds the day Vic had begun his illegal stay with me, but I could still see through the crack.

Trevor.

With a curse, I turned to Vic. "Go out back and hide again," I hissed. "It's Trevor! And do not step foot inside this house until I come and get you."

He rose from the couch and ran to the back door sounding like a herd of elephants. Trevor knocked on the front again, then rang the bell.

"I'm coming!" I yelled through the cacophony of dogs. When I heard the back door shut, I took a deep breath and tried to pull myself together.

My hand shook as I reached for the doorknob. Was he here to search for Vic again? And if yes, what would happen to our deal of working together? My nervousness quickly faded, replaced by curiosity. Was Trevor about to bust both Vic and me?

I flung open the door. His lip twisted up into a grin. "Hey," he said. "Did you get my text?"

My phone had been going off while I was talking to Vic. After pulling it from my pocket, I realized Trevor had indeed been texting me.

"Sorry, no, I didn't realize it. Do you want to come in?"

Pursing his lips, he hesitated for a long moment. "Make sure Vic is out of sight, okay? If I see him, I need to bring him in."

"He's not here," I said firmly. Trevor rolled his eyes in response.

"Come in," I muttered, not bothering to argue or attempt to convince him. My charade was up, and it appeared Trevor had definitely teamed up with me.

The dogs stopped him as he entered and sniffed his feet. After a moment, they decided he passed the test and allowed him to come farther into the house.

"Doing some repairs?" he asked, eyeing the bag of hinges, door locks, and miscellaneous other things sitting on the living room table.

"Yes," I said. "Lots of little things."

"Need any help?"

I gestured him to sit where Vic had been, then sent up a silent prayer that my brother would listen for once in his life and stay put under the house.

"No, I think I'm okay, but I appreciate the offer."

"Let me know if there's something I can do."

"Well, you could solve the mystery of who killed Phoebe," I said. "That would be helpful."

He chuckled and shook his head. "Doing my best, Gina. Doing my best."

I sighed and sat back against the cushions, then pushed my glasses up my nose. Daisy had gone M.I.A. after clearing Trevor to come inside. Then I realized I hadn't heard her speaking to me since we arrived home. Usually she had a lot to say about someone at the door. "So, why are you here?" I asked.

"I looked up that number on that text that was supposedly from Vic," he said. "I thought it would be best for me to come over and talk about it."

"Why couldn't you just call?" I asked.

"I'm trying to keep any indication that I'm not fully on board with Vic being the killer from Mallory."

"I see." But I had the distinct feeling he was lying to me, yet I had no idea what his ulterior motive could be. "So what's the big secret?"

"It's a secondary phone, one that wasn't in our records when I originally looked for it."

"Who did it belong to?" I asked.

"It's a burner you can buy at any gas station. There's no way to trace the number."

I'd figured as much. A killer wouldn't be stupid enough to use his or her own phone to frame my brother. "There's no way to find out any information on it?"

Trevor shook his head. "None."

"Then call it," I said. "Call it and let's see who answers."

"I don't think that's a good idea."

"Then give me the number," I said. "I'll call."

"Gina, you aren't thinking this through. It's not smart."

With a sigh, I crossed my arms over my chest. "Why?"

"Because if we call, then we're alerting the killer that we're on to them. They can ditch the phone and get rid of any other evidence they may be hiding. We're going to need any and all evidence to build a case. I can't compromise that."

Okay, he had a valid point. My goal had been to find who killed Phoebe and get Vic out of my hair. I hadn't given much thought to anything beyond that.

"This is so irritating," I muttered.

"That's policework," Trevor said. "It can be very frustrating."

We sat in silence for a long moment, then I had an idea that bordered on brilliance. "Let me see the phone number." I held out my hand.

"You can't call it, Gina. Besides, you've already looked at it."

"I looked at it, but I didn't memorize it. I promise I won't call it. I want to see if I recognize it. I have a lot of phone numbers because of my business, so I wanted to see if it would match up to any of them in my phone."

"You think the killer is getting their nails done at your salon?" he asked.

"It wouldn't be the first time." I waited for him to produce the number. When he didn't, I said, "Come on, Trevor. You have to start trusting me at some point."

He muttered something unintelligible, then pulled out a piece of paper from his pocket. "I wrote it down."

After taking the paper, I studied the number. It was local, but I didn't recognize it. I pulled out my phone and scrolled through my contacts, hoping for a match.

Trevor sat in silence, his stare boring into me. I committed the number to memory with the intention of putting it into my phone after he'd left, just so I'd have it. I handed him back the paper.

"Anything?" he asked.

I shook my head. "You do have to admit, it was a heck of an idea, though."

He grinned and sat back against the cushions, obviously relieved I'd kept my word and not dialed. "It actually was. I'm impressed."

A slow blush crawled over my cheeks. "Thanks. Every now and then I'm the smartest one in the room."

He laughed and I tried to figure out our next step.

"What do you think, Gina?" Trevor asked after a long moment.

I refocused on him and noted the blond stubble along his jawline. It looked cute on him.

"Honestly, I'm not sure what to think," I replied. "It seems like a lot of work to get a burner phone to set someone up for murder."

"I agree, Sherlock. And based on that fact alone, I believe we need to look at Chase very closely."

"Why is that?"

"From what I know of Chase, he's a very smart guy. Keeps the books for the ranch, as well as the schedule. He's very methodical, according to Roger Wagner."

The owner of the company would be aware of his employees' strongest attributes. "I think you're right," I said. "Buying a burner phone to set someone up for murder requires planning. He'd have to get the phone, get into Phoebe's, and set up the bogus number under my brother's name. Methodical and smart, indeed."

"I agree," Trevor said, standing and clasping his hands together. "So, when should we head out to the ranch?"

"T-together?" I stammered. I hadn't expected we'd be showing ourselves in public, a united front to catch a killer.

"Yes, Gina," he sighed. "Together. Two is always better than one when confronting a potential killer."

CHAPTER 15

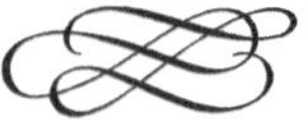

TREVOR and I agreed he would pick me up that night after dark. I watched through the blinds until he had driven away, then went outside to fetch my brother from under the house. For the rest of the day, Vic puttered around, completing the odd jobs I'd assigned him, while I spent some time writing and outlining. Thankfully, it was another productive writing session and my projects were on schedule.

Daisy had been awfully quiet, not even glancing up from the bed when I spoke to her.

"Are you not feeling well?" I asked,

gently stroking her head. She wouldn't even look at me. "Do you have a tummy ache?"

While I waited for an answer, a slight tinge of panic gripped my heart. Why wasn't she speaking to me? Did the fact I couldn't hear her mean that whatever wires had been crossed in my brain had somehow uncrossed, and now I was back to my version of normal?

I stroked Daisy's head for a few more minutes. "Do you want a treat? Maybe a piece of turkey?"

She closed her eyes.

"How about one of your favorite jerky sticks? I'll give you one, even though it gives you horrible gas."

No response.

"Daisy, what's going on? Can you give me some kind of sign here? Do you understand me?"

No tail wag, no quick lick of my fingers, and the worst part... no loving words.

I considered the past couple of days

and said, "I know you're mad because I haven't had a chance to walk you or pay much attention to you, but I need you to speak with me now."

She stood, stretched out her front legs as her butt rose in the air, then jumped off the bed and sauntered out of the room. A moment later, she barked. As I hurried into the kitchen, I found her at the back door waiting to be let out. Usually, she yelled for me in human language. As I opened the door, tears welled in my eyes. What in the world was going on?

Later that night, a light knock sounded at my front door. I exchanged glances with Vic, and he hurried into my son's room to make himself scarce. We decided that since Trevor knew I was hiding him and didn't seem to be too intent on doing anything about it, sending Vic under the house wasn't necessary.

I went to the front door and opened it to find Trevor, just as we'd agreed.

"You ready?" he asked.

I nodded, grabbed my bag and yelled

goodbye to the dogs, waiting to hear Daisy. Nothing. Only silence. After all this was over, I needed to concentrate on Daisy and figure out why I couldn't hear her any longer. My brow furrowed in worry. What if her voice had been in my head? What if I'd spent the last few months talking to myself, when I thought I'd been talking to the dog? A lot of soul searching would be necessary in the future, but I for now, needed to concentrate on finding Phoebe's killer.

Trevor and I had decided to visit the ranch at night because fewer people would be out and about and Vic had shared that most turned in very early since the day began at the crack of dawn.

As I slipped into Trevor's Jeep, I tried to recall the last time I'd ridden in a vehicle with a man who wasn't a family member, and I really struggled to recall. Perhaps on a dog rescuing mission? My life really seemed pathetic when I took a moment to examine it, so I decided to focus on other things.

Country music played softly from the speakers as we drove. I couldn't understand the lyrics, but I guessed the song was about a man's sorrow for the woman who left him, or a woman ready to bring hellfire on her cheating husband, and maybe something about beer and pickup trucks thrown in.

For some reason, I felt more and more nervous the further we drove. The need to fill the silence was strong, but I wasn't sure what to say. Besides that, I still didn't fully trust Trevor and I held on to the feeling that this stupid plan of working together would somehow backfire on me at some point.

We left Heywood and entered the forest. Darkness engulfed us on both sides, the only light being from the Jeep's headlights. If I stared at the street long enough, it felt as if we were in a tunnel. As always, I prayed the deer stayed in the trees.

"How was the rest of your day?" Trevor asked.

"Good. I got a lot done. What about you?"

"Not too bad," he said. "Some cows got loose over at the Tupper farm, so I went over there to help him wrangle them. Then I ended up spending a bit of time with the miniature goats he's got there." He shook his head and chuckled. "Cutest darn things I've ever seen."

I smiled as I tried to picture the hulking man next to me playing with miniature goats.

"One of them tried to eat my sunglasses," he continued. "Another got my shoelace. I couldn't even be mad, though. And the babies… don't get me started on them."

I'd heard of the goats at the Tupper farm from my friends, but hadn't been out to see them myself. It was my understanding that Charlie Tupper had built a small petting zoo for his grandkids, which, of course, included the goats. "Did you see the mini cows?" I asked. "He's got some of those as well."

"I didn't," Trevor replied. "And I'm really disappointed. Hopefully his other cattle will get out again sometime soon. I'll be on the lookout for the small cows if I get called out there."

He slowed and narrowed his gaze on the road. "The turnoff should be around here somewhere."

The road to Diamond Ranch was difficult to locate during the day. Under the darkness of night, it was nearly impossible. In fact, we drove by it, but then went up the highway a bit and turned around. We almost missed it the second time as well even with Siri telling us that we were right there.

As we drove down the dirt road, I glanced ahead, waiting for the big house to come into view. When it did, the sight took my breath away. A huge, yellow moon hung just above the building, making it seem small.

"That's some moon," Trevor whispered. "Haven't seen one like that in a long while."

I nodded in agreement. "I think I need to get out more, especially at night."

"Yeah, me too. That's really beautiful and shouldn't be missed."

We continued past the turn off leading to the house back to the employee cabins. Trevor pulled over under a tree and killed the headlights.

"Are we going to be in trouble for being here?" I asked as we were plunged into darkness. The moon should rise high in the sky very soon, lighting up the area.

"Nah. I think we'll be fine. We're just here to ask old Chase a few questions. It's not like we're going to rob anyone, unless you have other ideas."

We exited the vehicle and walked by the row of homes where Vic lived. "That's my brother's place," I whispered, pointing.

"I know," Trevor said. "I've been in there. We had to search it."

A reminder that he still didn't know I'd found what I perceived to be the murder weapon in Vic's closet, and I had no idea if it was put there before or after the search.

"When did you go through his things?" I asked. "Was it the day of the murder?"

Trevor nodded. "Right after you and Vic left the ranch."

"And… and you did the search yourself?"

"Yes, ma'am. Went through every nook and cranny of the dang place."

Either Trevor was incompetent, or the murder weapon had been placed after the search. I wanted the latter to be true so badly, I surprised myself. It was imperative that Trevor was a good guy, but I didn't fully understand why.

We continued our walk past the employee houses, as well as a pasture. I'd never been this far back on the property, and for a brief moment I wondered if Trevor had nefarious ideas. Was he taking me out to a pasture to kill me? And why in the world would I think such a thing?

"Chase's place is right up here," he said, pointing to an outline of a structure in the distance.

"So we just knock on his door and say hello?" I asked.

"Pretty much. Watch for body language cues, hear what he has to say."

I thought of all the times I'd snuck through the darkness of night to commit trouble. Lots of toilet papering my friends'—and a few enemies'—houses, sneaking out of my home to go to parties in the woods, and oftentimes, just to be out when I knew I shouldn't be. I'd never been nervous or afraid then, but I should've been. Wolves, coyotes and many other dangerous creatures populated the forest around Heywood. Bad people were out doing bad things at night. Yes, I should've been terrified, but the ignorance of youth had kept the thought of potential threats at bay.

As my palms became sweaty while we walked toward Chase's house, I realized the bravery of youth had fled. Even though my accomplice was a man of the law and he'd assured me we weren't doing anything illegal, I still wanted to go home and snuggle with my dogs.

Suddenly, I caught a glimpse of someone coming from the left. I tapped Trevor's shoulder and pointed. He grabbed me around the waist, lifted me off the ground, and we melted into the shadows of the trees. We dropped to our knees and I squinted as I tried to make out who the incoming person was, and did my utmost not to become irritated Trevor had handled me like a child.

"Why are we hiding?" I whispered.

"That's Cynthia Wagner," he replied. I squinted harder and wondered if I needed a new prescription, if my glasses were dirty, or if Trevor possessed some bat-like nighttime vision.

"It looks like she's going to Chase's," he continued. "I wonder why?"

"Well, he does run the farm for them," I said. "Maybe to discuss business?"

As Cynthia knocked on Chase's door, my stomach turned. I really, really wanted to go home.

"And I'm sorry about picking you up like that," Trevor said. "I wanted to get us out of her sight. It was a reflex."

"I understand. Just don't make a habit of it."

"Well, making a habit of it would require you and me to hang out a bit more. Are you up for that?"

I wasn't sure how to answer, so instead, I pointed to the house. "Let's go see what these two are doing."

We slowly walked toward the small cabin. Once we were at its side we both placed our backs to it and continued creeping until we could see into the window, which also happened to be open about an inch.

I crouched down right below it and hoped those inside didn't hear my knees popping.

"Cynthia!" Chase said. "What a surprise!"

"Yes, I was hoping you had time to go over the budget for the month. We'll need to make some cuts, and I wanted to get your input on where."

"Do you think they're talking really loud?" Trevor asked.

Now that he'd pointed it out, I nodded.

The door clicked shut, then Cynthia said, "Goodness, what a day."

"Come here," Chase growled. "Let me make it better for you."

Silence ensued, and I slowly raised my head to find them in a passionate embrace, lip-locked. Bile rose in my throat as I lowered myself back onto my haunches.

"Are they doing what I think they're doing?" Trevor whispered.

I grimaced and nodded.

"Gross."

No argument there. We waited a few moments, then Chase said, "Have you heard any more about Phoebe's investigation?"

"I spoke to Sheriff Richards today, and it seems they're still focused on Vic."

Chase chuckled as I glared at Trevor, who simply shrugged.

"I hope they catch him soon," Chase muttered.

"Me, too," Cynthia said. "But I must admit, it's nice for everyone to get what they want."

"It is. I never imagined I'd finally get promoted."

"Oh, come on, Chase," Cynthia chided. "I told you it would all work out. Now, are you done talking, or are we going to go over this budget?"

"I always work best in the bedroom," Chase said.

"Yes, you do."

I looked at Trevor as they moved through the small house. The bedroom light turned on for a moment, then went dark.

"Please don't say we're going to stay for the rest of this," I whispered.

Trevor shook his head. "We came to talk to Chase, but I think we got much more information than any conversation could bring."

"Agreed." But I wasn't sure how it all fit together.

"Let's go," he said.

We crept back the way we came and hurried to the car. After he'd started the engine, and we were on the dirt road leading out to the highway, he spoke. "I think I need a beer. Feeling a little sickly after listening to that."

"I'm with you there." I also felt dirty, like a shower was in order. As we turned onto the highway, a thought occurred to me. If I already felt dirty, maybe it would be a good time to visit Hold Your Horses, the dive bar just a few miles away. Chances were great we'd catch Debbie Towerhall and ask her about her violent past, her relationship with my brother, and Phoebe's demise.

CHAPTER 16

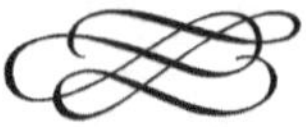

"I'D RATHER PLAY Russian Roulette with a loaded gun then step foot in that place tonight," Trevor said in response to my idea.

"Yes, it's a terrible bar," I said. "But chances are greater than not that Debbie Towerhall is there, and we need to talk to her."

"You realize that a lot of people who go there are ones I've put away, right?" Trevor asked.

"Don't worry about it," I said. "You'll be with me."

He glanced over, his brow furrowed.

"Gina, no offense, but you're around five-foot-three and maybe a buck twenty-five after you've overeaten."

I nodded and smiled while tucking a lock of hair behind my ear. "All that may be true, but Vic's my brother. He's got something on every single person who may be in there, and his name carries weight with the lowlifes of Heywood. Trust me, you'll be fine."

Trevor cursed and shook his head. "So you're going to be my bodyguard?"

I snorted at the thought of little old me protecting the hulking sheriff. "If that's the way you want to think of it, then yes."

We drove in silence for another moment and I thought he'd speed right on past the bar. A small part of me hoped he would, but we did need to talk to Debbie, no matter how badly I'd rather skip the conversation. Instead, he said, "This I've got to see," then yanked the steering wheel to the left.

The parking lot was almost full. After finding a spot in the dirt lot, we walked to the door. Yes, I talked a big game and I knew no one would bother me because of my relation to Vic, but I wasn't sure if that protection would extend to Trevor. I certainly hoped so.

Hold Your Horses had been a staple in the area since Heywood's inception. The founders of Heywood had been somewhat of a religious group and didn't want the dredges of society partaking in their drinking within the town limits. So, someone had decided that they'd build a place just outside of said limits. Of course, all the restaurants in town now served alcohol, but the bar remained a place where one could go to find drugs and a fist fight, if so inclined. Besides his job at Diamond Ranch, it was my brother's favorite place to be.

I pushed open the door and was hit smack in the face with a wall of smoke and the Eagles' *Lying Eyes* blaring over the speakers. I glanced around through the haze and dim light. Every stool at the bar held a patron. A few people hung around the pool table. I noted all the tables had been taken, too.

"Time to belly up to the bar," I muttered. As we made our way through the crowd, people stared.

"What's that copper doing here?" I glanced to my right to find a big, burly biker eyeing Trevor. If I remembered correctly, Handlebar was his name, and he hailed from Sedona's biker gang.

Ah, the people I knew, thanks to my brother. "Leave him alone, dude. He's with me."

Handlebar studied Trevor one last time, then nodded.

Trevor leaned over. "I'm impressed," he whispered in my ear.

Whatever. I wished I had never suggested this nonsense and went home to discover if my dog was talking to me again or if my brain had somehow returned to "normal" mode without me realizing it.

I sidled up to the bar and stared at the bartender until we made eye contact. "Gina!" she shouted. I smiled as my old high school friend, Rainy, hurried over. "I haven't seen you in months!"

"You're right," I said, giving her a quick hug over the bar.

"Where's Vic?" she asked. Grey curly hair pushed back with a red and blue bandanna sprung out around her head like a halo. Thick lines creased at her eyes while two dove tattoos peeked out of her blouse.

"I don't know," I lied. "I haven't seen him in days."

Trevor grunted behind me, but I ignored him.

"We haven't either," Rainy pouted. "I miss the turd. What's with all that nonsense at the ranch? Do the police really think he could've killed Phoebe?"

I glanced over my shoulder then back at Rainy. Her eyes widened as she stared at Trevor.

"Hey, Rainy," he yelled over the din. "Nice to see you again."

"You never come in here unless I call for you," she said. "What are you doing here? The place is pretty mellow tonight."

"Just along for the ride with Gina," he said.

"We're looking to speak with Debbie Towerhall," I said. "Have you seen her?"

Rainy arched an eyebrow, then hitched a thumb to her left. I followed it until I found exactly who I'd been looking for.

Debbie Towerhall.

Long, curly black hair fell down her back as she swayed to the music with both arms above her head, a beer bottle in one hand.

"Don't tell her I sent you over," Rainy said. "She's in a mood tonight."

"Isn't she in a mood every night?" I asked.

"Yeah, but tonight's particularly bad. She's either trying to go home with someone or get into a scuffle. I haven't decided which."

Wonderful. Hopefully I could manage a peaceful conversation with her.

After taking a deep breath, I snaked through the crowd and tapped her shoulder. She turned around and stared at me a long moment with glassy eyes as if she couldn't recall my name. Then, the proverbial lightbulb went off and a smile was quickly replaced with a grimace.

"What do you want?" she asked. Apparently, her dislike of my brother had been extended to me.

Dressed in jeans and a black tank top, she looked older than her forty-something years. Deep lines framed her mouth and eyes. Her life decisions hadn't been kind.

"I wanted to talk to you about Vic," I said.

"What about him?" she asked. "Please give me the wonderful news of his death, preferably a long, painful one."

With a smile, I shook my head. "Sorry to disappoint you, but no."

"Then what do you want?" she asked again.

"Well, I understand he left you to try to win back Phoebe."

She snorted and shook her head. "Bad move on his part." Her gaze narrowed as she looked over my shoulder. "Why are the cops here?"

"He's helping me with something," I said.

"Nice tat, Debbie," Trevor commented, pointing at her forearm. "Is it new? I don't recall seeing it the last time we met."

I glanced down at her arm. It read, *Their Is No Love.* I ground my jaw at the grammar issue, but decided to bring the conversation back on track. She either didn't care, or she hadn't figured out the epic, permanent mistake quite yet.

"Tell me more about the breakup, Debbie," I urged. "I'd really like to know the details."

"Vic and I had a really good thing going," she said. "Really good. We were like Bonnie and Clyde."

I nodded, realizing that Debbie had put far more stock in the relationship than Vic had. She had been a distraction to him, someone to take his mind off the pain of Phoebe leaving him. He'd been a lot more to Debbie, though.

"That must have hurt when he broke it off," I ventured.

"It did. But I got my revenge."

I traded glances with Trevor. "What does that revenge look like?" he asked.

"I don't talk to cops," Debbie spat, then took a long pull from her beer bottle.

"Then talk to me," I said. "What did you do to get your revenge?"

As she swayed, her eyes seemed to have trouble focusing. For a second, I was afraid she was going to pass out and I'd have to come back another time to talk to her. I'd rather play that Russian Roulette Trevor mentioned.

I grabbed her shoulders. "Debbie, what revenge did you get on Vic?"

All I wanted was for her to admit she'd killed Phoebe. Trevor could then arrest her, and I could go home and kick Vic out of my house.

Instead, she balled a fist and hit me square in the chin.

Dang it. I should've seen that one coming. After all, I was speaking with Debbie

Towerhall. The same woman who stabbed her last boyfriend and was in and out of jail more than Vic was.

I released her shoulders and staggered backward while a few stars appeared before my eyes. Why in the world had I bothered with this nonsense?

Trevor and Debbie screamed at each other as I gathered my bearings. The sound of chairs scraping filled the air as someone yelled, "Fight!"

My first instinct was to leave the horrible bar, but then my childhood lessons kicked into gear. Before I knew what I was doing, I lunged at Debbie, my shoulder plowing into her stomach. As I lifted her over my shoulder and planted her on the floor behind me, the bar exploded into cheers and shouts of approval. I turned around, pounced on her to straddle her, and held her hand above her head. "What was your revenge?" I shouted over the din of the crowd that had now gathered around us, forming a tight circle.

She laughed and shook her head. "My revenge is that I beat up his sister!"

As she continued to cackle, Trevor laid a hand on my forearm. "Let's go, Gina."

I glanced up at him and read worry in his gaze as it darted around the bar. He was right. The situation could turn worse than it already was within seconds.

Focusing my attention back to Debbie, I said, "That's it? That's the big revenge? You trying to get the upper hand on me?"

I slowly released her wrists as she continued to laugh, and I realized the whole visit to Hold Your Horses had been an epic waste of time.

Trevor helped me to my feet as I fought the urge to give Debbie a hard kick to the ribs.

"Let's get out of here," he muttered as he led me through the crowd, his hand firmly wrapped around my bicep. We were met with people upset there hadn't been a good old-fashioned girl fight at the bar.

"Vic's going to be disappointed," Handlebar said. "You should've knocked her out cold."

"Oh, shut up," I snarled while Trevor pushed me from behind toward the door.

The fresh air jarred me almost as much as Debbie's fist had. I inhaled deeply and shut my eyes.

"Are you okay?" Trevor asked.

"I'm fine," I mumbled. "Just take me home."

As we walked to his Jeep, he said, "I'm impressed, Gina."

I remained silent as I slipped into the vehicle. Once inside, I gently prodded my chin with my fingers. Probably a bruise, but not a serious injury.

"Are you okay?" Trevor asked again. "Do you need medical attention?"

"No," I sighed. "Nothing that a glass of wine and a bag of peas won't cure."

We drove out of the parking lot, and I replayed the conversation with Debbie. "I think it's safe to say she didn't have anything to do with Phoebe's murder."

"You may be right. Either that, or she was trying to distract you with her attack."

"Maybe." I really didn't think Debbie was that smart, especially with the evidence tattooed on her arm. Anyone who allowed that had rocks for brains, or maybe in Debbie's case, beer.

Despite what had happened, I was much more interested in Chase as a suspect.

With Phoebe's death, he got his promotion and his lover, Cynthia, got rid of her husband's girlfriend. If she was sleeping with Chase, I couldn't imagine why she'd care if her husband was cheating.

But then again, maybe I had misjudged Debbie. Perhaps Trevor was right and she was smarter than I gave her credit for. If that was true, she had to realize that if she killed Phoebe, Vic wouldn't return to her. Right?

Or maybe, she was just stupid enough to believe that he would.

CHAPTER 17

WHEN WE PULLED up in front of the house, Trevor glanced over at me. "I'll see you later, okay?"

"Just come in," I said, rolling my eyes. "We need to talk about everything."

"What about Vic?" he asked. "I'm supposed to take him in if I see him, and I have a feeling if I walk through that door, I'll do just that."

I sighed as my chin began to throb. "You can pretend you don't see him. It's probably a good idea for the three of us to hash all this out and have his input."

Trevor sighed. "Okay. I won't arrest him."

"Frankly, I really don't care if you do or don't," I replied. "I'm really tired of being in the middle of all his drama."

We exited the car and I hurried to the front door. The dogs barked as I jammed my key into the lock. They quieted and sniffed me once I stepped inside. I listened intently for Daisy's voice, but was met with silence. She did stare up at me with that wide brown gaze while wagging her tail, so she didn't seem too mad at me, but I sure wished she would speak to me.

I found Vic in the living room sprawled out on the couch with Sing lying on his stomach and chest. They were watching an old western movie.

"Hey, Gina," he greeted me, then took a sip of what I could only guess was the remnants of my whisky. When Trevor walked in behind me, Vic's eyes widened. "What the heck!" he yelled. "You brought the cops in to arrest me?"

Sing barked and whined.

"Don't tempt me," I snarled. "I'd love nothing more than to send you to prison right now, but he's here to help us, so relax."

"Go get your peas and wine," Trevor said.

"What does she need peas for?" Vic asked as I hurried to the kitchen.

"Your girlfriend took a swing at her," Trevor said.

"Who? I don't have a girlfriend."

"Let me clarify for you: Debbie sucker punched Gina," Trevor replied.

"Are you kidding me?" Vic asked. I pulled the bag of peas out of the freezer and the bottle of wine out of the fridge. After I poured a glass, I returned to the living room and sat down next to Trevor. Vic hadn't budged. "Debbie hit you?"

I rested the bag of frozen peas on my chin. "Yes, she did."

A string of curses fell from his lips as he struggled to sit up. Sing finally relented and allowed it. "I hope you didn't take it from her," Vic said.

"Of course not," I muttered.

"She dished it out a lot harder than Debbie did," Trevor said, eyeing me with a smile. "It was something to see, Vic. This girl can take care of herself."

"Yeah, I made sure of that," Vic grumbled. "But me and Debbie are going to have some words."

And that couldn't happen until I got him out of my house. If he showed his face in public, he'd go to jail. Yes, I was furious that he'd put me in this situation and that I hadn't seen Debbie's fist coming, but in my heart, I didn't want him put away for something he didn't do. We needed to find the murderer, and once he was in the clear, he could leave and go have words with Debbie. "I don't think she killed Phoebe," I said. "But did you know Chase and Cynthia are sleeping together?"

Vic's mouth fell open. "You're joking."

"Afraid not," Trevor replied. "We definitely got more than we bargained for while trying to speak to Chase."

"What happened?" Vic asked. As we shared the story, his gaze bounced between the two of us while he sipped the whisky. "I had no idea. I'd never believe it if you hadn't heard and seen it for yourselves."

"Why is that?" Trevor asked.

"Because Cynthia is a churchgoer. She tries to get the rest of us down to Minister Paul's every Sunday. Drives everyone crazy. But isn't that a rule in the church? Don't mess around on your spouse?"

"I think that's a good rule for everyone, regardless of faith," Trevor said.

As someone who had once been married to a serial cheater and wife beater, I agreed wholeheartedly.

Minister Paul ran the church in town, a beautiful stone structure that had been built when Heywood was discovered hundreds of years ago. It had been Catholic but was now non-denominational and all were welcome to pray there. The church stayed pretty busy, mainly because of Minister Paul. In his late twenties with a head of black hair, a strong jawline and magnetic personality, the women of Heywood adored him. He'd never lacked for a flock that I'd seen. The parking lot brimmed with vehicles every Sunday.

"A lot of us at the ranch aren't the churchgoing type," Vic continued. "We need to make ourselves invisible on Sunday because she'll come and knock on our doors to try to get us to go."

As I pressed the peas to my face and sipped my wine, I mulled the dichotomy of Cynthia Wagner—a married woman of faith who slept with her employee. Or was there more than one? If so, Vic would be high on the list, especially with his good looks. "Did you and Cynthia ever... you know?" I asked.

"Heck no." Vic grimaced. "Give me some credit. I wouldn't touch Cynthia with a ten-foot pole."

I shrugged. "You tangled with Debbie. I

think she's a few notches down from Cynthia."

Vic glared at me as I gave him a sweet smile. "Alright, that's fair," he grumbled. "You aren't going to let me live that one down, are you?"

"Nope."

He leaned back against the cushions and stared at the ceiling. "I never should've told you."

"Nope. But you did, and now you must live with the consequences of my never-ending reminders of just how low you've stooped. And I plan to bring it up often."

"You're heartless, Gina."

"Yes," I sighed. "I most certainly can be."

"Okay, I love the sibling banter, but let's get back to solving this murder." Trevor chuckled.

"Don't you have siblings?" I asked. "A brother or sister who irritates you to no end?"

"Can't say that I do." He shook his head and laced his fingers together in his lap.

"I've got one younger sister I don't talk to and an older brother who died."

"Why don't you talk to your sister?" Vic asked.

"That's none of your business," Trevor said. Although he was smiling, he'd made it very clear a line had been drawn and Vic was not to cross it.

I tried to imagine cutting Vic out of my life. Heaven knew he sometimes deserved it, and a lot of times I really wanted an existence free of his escapades and drama. But I couldn't comprehend my life without him, no matter how much he irritated me. We were bonded in that familial way that couldn't be broken.

As for Trevor's dead brother, I supposed that would be a story for another time, if I was ever privy to it. Even though we'd grown up in the same town, I didn't recall his older brother dying, or his younger sister even existing.

Trevor obviously wanted to get the conversation back on track to Phoebe's murder. Not that I blamed him. Dealing with tricky family relationships could be difficult to navigate for those involved and impossible for outsiders to understand.

"Yes," I said. "Let's get back to the big question: Who killed Phoebe?"

We sat in silence for a long moment. No one had an answer.

"Can I get a whisky?" Trevor asked.

I glanced at my glass, then Vic's. We were hopelessly rude. I often wondered if we'd grown up with a mother, we'd both be different. "I'm sorry," I said. "I should've offered you something."

"There's still some whisky left," Vic said, absently stroking Sing's head. "But you'll need to get some more at the store tomorrow."

I hurried to the kitchen. After placing the peas back in the freezer, I poured Trevor the last of the whisky, refilled my wine, then returned to the living room.

"Nothing for me?" Vic asked.

"That's it. You drank it all."

Trevor took the glass from me and downed the amber liquid in one long drink. As he set down the glass on the table, he smiled, obviously happy he'd gotten the upper hand on Vic.

Both sat back against the cushions and sighed in unison. Maybe they had more in common than either realized.

"So who killed Phoebe?" I asked again.

Vic turned his stare to Trevor. "What did you see on the cameras?"

A long pause ensued before Trevor asked, "What cameras?"

"The cameras on the property!" Vic yelled, shooting to his feet.

Trevor rubbed his hands together and stood. "Again, what cameras, Vic?"

"No one told you about the cameras?" Vic asked incredulously, spreading his arms wide. "Are you kidding me?"

They stared at each other a long moment, then Trevor shook his head. "I haven't heard about any cameras."

Vic cursed again and sat down, placing his elbows on his knees, his head in his hands.

"Tell me, Vic. Where are the cameras?" Trevor asked.

"All over the property," he replied. "Sometimes they work, sometimes they don't." My heart thundered and I took a large gulp of wine No one had told the cops about the cameras?

"You know what that means," Vic continued.

Trevor and I traded glances, and he nodded. "It's someone who works at Diamond Ranch. Someone who knows about the cameras, but doesn't want the sheriff's department to be aware of them."

"Or the cameras weren't working at the time, and they didn't see a reason to tell anyone," I said.

Both glared at me.

"I feel like you're conspiring against me," Vic grumbled.

"No," I replied. "Simply pointing out there's another way to look at this situation."

"I think someone there is hiding something," Trevor growled. "And that really upsets me."

Glancing down at Daisy who had curled at my feet, I pursed my lips. How did I tell Vic and Trevor that Daisy had smelled Buck at the crime scene without mentioning that I could speak—or just yesterday I *could* speak—to my dog, but not now? He didn't work at the farm, but his scent had been detected there. However, Vic had also said that Buck had visited the farm in the previous couple of days before Phoebe's death, and I had no way of questioning Daisy to see if a scent would last that long.

She glanced up at me and gave a quick tail wag, then closed her eyes again.

"I need to get back to the station and see if I missed the part where someone at the ranch told me about those dang cameras," Trevor said. "Thanks for the interesting night, Gina."

"Of course," I said. "Thank you for... well, I'm not sure what to thank you for since I was exposed to some weird sex stuff and a fist to the face, but I guess I feel better with you on our side."

Trevor threw his head back and laughed. Vic joined in. I prodded my bruised jaw.

I stood and escorted Trevor to the door, wondering how in the world I was going to communicate with the canine who had the answers I needed to my burning questions.

CHAPTER 18

AFTER GOING TO BED, I spent two hours trying to get Daisy to speak with me as I rubbed her belly. She groaned with pleasure but had nothing to say.

"Daisy, I just need to know if Buck's scent would stay on the dirt for two days," I whispered. "Can you please just tell me that? Help me out a little?"

Instead of the answer I hoped for, her tongue lolled out the side of her mouth, then she sighed and closed her eyes.

I stared at the ceiling while listening to her soft snores, my mind spinning with desperation. After my son, Jacob, had left for college, Daisy had been more than just my dog—she'd been my companion and I hadn't felt so lonely. Of course, she was special because she could speak. But had all the conversations and all the jokes we'd shared been figments of my imagination? At this point, it sure seemed that was the case. As the claws of loneliness once again ripped at my chest, tears welled in my eyes. I urgently wanted her to talk to me again. I *needed* her.

When my phone buzzed on my night-stand, my loneliness turned to worry. A call this late was never good news. I sat up in bed and grabbed the device, becoming almost frantic when I realized it was Jacob.

"Jacob?" I answered. "Are you okay?"

"Hey, Mom," he said. "I'm fine. Were you sleeping?"

Did I detect a little sadness in his voice? "No, I wasn't. What's up, honey?"

"Well, I was wondering if I could come home this weekend."

I leaned against the pillows and smiled,

my heart bursting with joy. "Of course you can," I said measuredly. I didn't want him to know just how much the plan excited me. "You don't have to ask, Jacob."

"Okay, cool. One of the guys in my dorm said he's driving by Heywood on his way to Sedona, and he'll drop me off."

"Wonderful. I'm looking forward to seeing you."

But then I remembered Vic was camped out in Jacob's room. He'd simply have to move to the couch if we hadn't caught the murderer by then. How did I explain to my son that his uncle was wanted for killing his ex-girlfriend and I was breaking the law by allowing him to stay at my home?

I'd figure it out later.

"Is everything okay there?" I asked. "Are you having fun? Learning anything?"

"Yeah, probably too much fun," he said. "I learned to beer bong, and English isn't too bad."

"Well, beer-bonging is an important life skill."

"It is not," Jacob said, laughing. "When was the last time you had a beer bong?"

"Probably when I was your age," I replied. "But I'm glad English is interesting."

He sighed. "I'm really tired. My dorm is party central and I just wanted to get away for a few days."

I'd never gone to college, but I had done some serious partying in my late teens / early twenties. I understood exactly where my son was coming from, especially since he was somewhat introverted.

"Will you be home on Friday?" I asked.

"That's the plan. Probably about noon or so."

"We'll have some steaks Friday night," I replied, mentally making a grocery list. "We can barbecue."

"That sound great, Mom. I'm eating a bunch of junk food here."

"When you come home, we'll get you brimming with some of the good stuff."

"Thanks," he said. "Looking forward to seeing you."

"Same here, honey. I can't wait until Friday!"

After I hung up, I set down my phone and smiled. Jacob was coming home! I had to hit the grocery store and also figure out a way to tell him about the quandary with Vic.

Even though Jacob's father had only died a little over a year ago, he hadn't been a big figure in his son's life. His lack of contributions, both financial and emotional, had left Jacob and me plowing through the years together—the dynamic duo. He had been a good kid—never in trouble, an easygoing demeanor, and always willing to help around the house. Our relationship reminded me more of a friendship than a parent-child dynamic.

I couldn't wait to see him.

"Jacob's coming home, Daisy," I whispered into the dark.

She remained quiet, but I heard the thump of her tail hitting the mattress.

Apparently, we were all excited.

I ROSE the next morning with the sun while Daisy remained in bed. After a quick shower, I hurried into the kitchen to find Vic brewing a pot of his version of coffee, or as I liked to call it, his sludge. Banshee eyed me from her spot by the food bowl while Sing lay under the table, his gaze never leaving Vic. The dog was obviously smitten and I hoped my stupid brother didn't break his heart.

"Jacob's coming home," I said.

"That's great!" Vic exclaimed. "Can't wait to see my nephew and hear about his life in college!"

"He'll be here Friday," I continued. "I was thinking we'd barbecue some steaks along with some potato salad and corn on the cob."

"Count me in. Just listening to you is causing my stomach to growl."

"You need to move out of his room."

"And where am I going to sleep?" Vic asked.

"Under the house, for all I care, but my kid is getting his room back. From what he told me last night, he needs some peace and quiet."

Vic chuckled and nodded. "Noted. Maybe you'll have caught the killer by then and I'll be out of your hair."

"Wouldn't that be great?"

He rolled his eyes. "Trust me, Gina. I don't like living here. I'm going stir crazy thinking about my horses at the ranch and wondering how their training is going and who took over, if anyone. Phoebe and I were the best ones, so I'm a little worried."

I sipped my coffee. I had to remember this arrangement was difficult for him as well. I put a little more water and creamer into the sludge, hoping to make it somewhat palatable.

"And you know I like to be in motion," he continued. "This sitting around indoors all day is making me crazy."

"Did you finish all the jobs I had for

you?"

"Almost."

I wracked my brain trying to come up with something else for him to do. "You could always catch up on your soap operas."

He furrowed his brow. "I'd rather get run over by a tractor."

With a smile, I set down my cup. "I'm headed to the grocery store to get stuff for when Jacob visits. Do you want anything?"

"Whisky."

"Anything else?"

While he listed his grocery wishes, I pulled out my phone and typed up the list. It was going to be one heck of a large bill at the store.

"Can you feed the dogs for me?" I asked as I gathered my purse.

"Sure."

"Daisy won't be up for a couple of hours, so make sure to pull her food or Banshee will eat it."

"Right."

"I'll see you later."

My mood hadn't been this light in a long time. With a little spring in my step and a smile I couldn't tame, I felt like a million bucks. And because of that, I decided to treat myself to a proper cup of coffee at the local coffee shop, Cup of Go.

To make my day even better, I found a parking spot right in front. The line was short, the barista friendly and she fetched my Americano quickly. With my java in hand, I drove down to Timber Trades, the town grocery store, where I again found a parking spot with ease.

According to Heywood history, the building used to be a place where people would come to make trades before modern civilization took over. Milk for wood. Vegetables for meat. When it became a grocery store, they'd never changed the name.

Once inside, I found the fresh corn, picked up some fixings for a green salad, and grabbed a tub of potato salad. For a short moment, I considered making my own, but quickly shoved that idea aside. I could count on the store-bought one tasting pretty good. With my own recipe, it was hit or miss.

As I strode over to the butcher, I hummed along with David Bowie's *Let's Dance* piped into the store speakers. Annabelle loved shopping at Timber Trades because she often heard her favorites.

My smile faded as I rounded the corner. Roger Wagner, the owner of Diamond Ranch, stood at the counter.

Narrowing my gaze, I debated whether to speak to him or not. If I brought up the cameras, he could rush back to the ranch and erase them. However, I could also use it as a tactic to flush him out. Maybe he'd become really upset and drop me a clue as to whether he'd intentionally not mentioned the cameras to the police, or he'd simply forgotten. I decided to take my chances since Trevor was only a phone call away. Relaying the information I discovered would be easy.

I strode up to Roger and tapped him on

the shoulder. When he glanced down, I smiled. "Remember me?"

Pursing his lips, he furrowed his brow as if he couldn't quite recall. Suddenly, his gaze widened. "You're Vic's sister!"

"Bingo!" I exclaimed. "You get a prize!"

"Where's your brother?" he asked. "The police are looking for him!"

"I have no idea," I replied, shrugging. "If he was smart, he'd be long gone to avoid the sheriff railroading him, but that's just what I'd do."

"You'd break the law?"

"Heck, yes," I replied. "If I didn't do anything wrong I most certainly would. Us Dunners don't like to go to prison for crimes we don't commit."

"He killed Phoebe," he said, wagging his finger in my face.

I slapped it away. I hated when people talked down to me. "Well, let's go to your big old ranch and take a look at the footage from cameras you've got every-where. How about that? Then we can have a discussion on who *really* killed her."

His face paled as he stepped away from me. Obviously, he hadn't expected me to have this knowledge. "Caught you by surprise there, didn't I?"

"T-the cameras aren't working," he stammered.

"Is that why you didn't tell the police about them?" I asked. I leaned in and whispered, "They're coming for the cameras, Roger. And they know you lied."

"I haven't lied!" he said. "The cameras aren't working!"

"Well, the police are going to find out whether that's true or not."

I smiled, enjoying watching his gaze dart all around the store as he quickly processed the implications. When he raced past me and out the door, I chuckled. Based on his reaction, I was pretty sure I'd just discovered the killer. I pulled out my phone and dialed Trevor. After sharing my conversation with Roger, I said, "You better get over there before he destroys all the cameras and erases any footage he may have."

"I'm already on my way," Trevor said. "He won't arrive before me."

After hanging up, I shoved the phone back in my pocket. Could my day get any better? It seemed we were really close to getting Vic out of my house, just in time for Jacob to come home.

I picked out the best-looking ribeye steaks, grabbed a few other items, paid, then headed out to my car while humming David Bowie, which had stuck with me after hearing it in the store.

As I loaded my groceries into the trunk, an arm snaked around my neck. With a gasp, I grabbed the forearm and tried to wrench away from my attacker. A scream got stuck in my throat when I felt an awful pain in my side just below my ribs. Within seconds, my muscles went slack and all fight left me as I dangled in my assailant's hold.

I fought to keep my eyes open, but lost. My last worry before darkness engulfed me—I feared I'd never see Jacob again.

CHAPTER 19

CONSCIOUSNESS CAME SLOWLY. The first thing I noticed was the smell of hay. My legs also itched. I opened one eye and glanced around, wondering why I was lying in a pile of straw, but the question was too complex for me to answer.

I faded to blackness.

When I peeled my eyes open again, it was dark. A sliver of light came through the slats of wood, possibly from the moon. Was that horse poop I smelled?

It was then I realized my hands were tied behind me and I had something over my mouth. Panic built in my chest, my breath coming in shortened spurts.

"Just breathe like you did when you were asleep, Gina."

I glanced around in the darkness for the owner of the voice and realized my glasses had been taken, which didn't bode well for me as I couldn't see three feet in front of my face without them. The voice was definitely male. Was it Roger Wagner? I'd certainly upset him in the store, but I thought he'd run back to the ranch to erase any evidence. Instead, he'd come for me. My panic only worsened while my breath sawed.

This is what it feels like to suffocate to death.

"If you relax, you'll be fine. Lie back, close your eyes, and chill out."

Although I hated being told what to do, I followed the instructions to hopefully avoid death. I squinted into the darkness. What sounded like a horse huffed on the other side of the wooden wall. Based on the hay, the horse and the warm, dusty air, I was definitely in a barn.

The voice, who I assumed was Roger, seemed to be coming from outside the stall.

Whatever he'd shot into me had upset my stomach and made me woozy. I felt as if I might throw-up, and with the tape over my mouth, I'd definitely suffocate. Going out choking on my own vomit wasn't the way I intended my life to end.

I rolled to my side and kicked the wooden slats. No answer. I slammed my heel into them again.

"Knock it off, Gina," he growled. "No one can hear you."

Ignoring him and the desperate tears sliding out the corner of my eyes, I kicked the planks until the door of the stall opened. I squinted to see a face, but knew who it was before he reached me. The smell of beer and body odor overwhelmed the area.

Buck.

The idiot had drugged and kidnapped

me, I assumed to get back at Vic for the money he owed.

"I said don't kick the walls, Gina." He squatted down about a foot away from me, then laughed. "With all that hay in your hair and dirt smudged on your face, you look like you just tangled with the Devil himself."

Hoping to convey I desperately needed the tape removed from my mouth, I began breathing hard again. My heart thundered and tears tracked down my face as I stared at him. Finally, he sighed and pulled the tape off me. After sucking in some deep breaths, I laid my head down and swore. The area around my mouth burned like fire and I hoped all my skin was still intact.

"Buck, you are dumber than I thought," I said. I rolled to my side and sat up again. Now that I could breathe, my stomach was settling, but my brain still felt like it had been dipped in fizzy mineral water.

"That's a good way to get that smart mouth taped up again."

"Sorry," I apologized. "I didn't mean that." Of course, I did, but I just couldn't deal with the tape again.

"So, what are we doing here?" I asked. Was I slurring? "What's the plan?"

"The plan is for you to stay quiet and for other people to work things out."

He stood and walked out the stable door, then shut it behind him.

Okay, so he wasn't going to kill me… at least not right away. Who were the people working things out? And what were the things? And how in the world did I fit into all this if it wasn't retribution for Vic not paying his bills?

I lay down again and tried to piece it all together, but my head felt like chocolate pudding had been piped in to replace my brain. I don't know how long I stared at the ceiling before I sat up and yelled for Buck.

"You need to keep quiet!" he hissed as he entered the stall with a shovel over his shoulder. He slammed it on the ground next to me. "I mean it, Gina!"

I stared at the indent where the metal plate had been as cold sweat tickled my skin, despite the warm air.

"Please stay here with me," I begged. "I'm… I'm afraid, Buck. I'm scared you're going to kill me, just like you said."

Did I really think he'd do it? Probably not, but I wanted answers, and the only way I was going to get them is if he kept talking.

"Then shut up!"

"I promise," I whispered. "Just don't leave me."

He stared at me a long moment, then shook his head. After throwing down the shovel in the corner, he sat down by the door. "Your brother was right," he snarled. "You *are* a pain in the butt."

I wasn't going to apologize for trying to stay alive.

"If you don't keep quiet, I'll drug you again," Buck said.

Okay, maybe another apology was in order. "I'm sorry. Please don't drug me or hit me with the shovel. You have to understand that I'm a bit upset right now. One minute I'm loading groceries into the car, then next, I'm tied up in a barn stall, and I don't know why."

He sighed and shook his head. "You should've let Vic take the fall for the murder, Gina. If you hadn't stuck your nose where it doesn't belong, you wouldn't be in this situation."

So this wasn't about the money Vic owed him? This was about Phoebe?

"I'm confused, Buck. Did you kill Phoebe?"

He glared at me and shook his head. "I'm not telling you anything, Gina." A small smile spread across his face. "If I did, then I'd have to break open your skull with the shovel."

At that point, I decided it was best for me to keep my mouth shut and try to think things through, except my brain didn't want to work.

Then I remembered Jacob was coming home for the weekend. No way was I going to be dead in a barn when my son returned from college.

"What did you drug me with?" I asked. Maybe if I got an answer there, I'd know how long I'd feel I had mush in my head.

"Horse tranquilizer," he replied. "A little bit goes a long way."

I'd learned when my ex died that the drug cartels were using horse tranquilizers while whipping up their recipes for human consumption. Buck had shot me full of opioids. Ugh. It could be hours before my system cleared the poison.

I also knew that Diamond Ranch had horse tranquilizers on hand. That fact, combined with the knowledge of me being held captive, had something to do with Phoebe's death. I had no doubt I was at the ranch, probably tucked away in one of the barns that wasn't used frequently.

Okay, so maybe my brain was working. At least I had a solid idea of where I was being stored. Next, I had to find a way out. Even if I didn't have the answers to all my questions, I had to escape. I could figure out the rest later.

Lying in the hay wasn't going to help me.

I pushed my legs so I scooted backward toward a wall. Buck eyed me curiously, his sinewy muscles tense as if he was ready to pounce.

"Just need to lean up against something," I said, giving him a small smile. "Relax, Buck. You've got me tied up. I'm not going anywhere."

When I reached the wall, I leaned against it and sighed for good measure. "My back feels better already."

I felt around behind me hoping for a nail. If I could find something sharp, maybe I could work the ropes against it and free myself. In the meantime, I had to keep him talking.

"A little birdie told me you were at the scene of Phoebe's death," I said.

He furrowed his brow. "Who told you that?"

"Like I said, a little birdie."

"Well, they're wrong. I wasn't around the night Phoebe was killed, and I can prove it."

"How would you do that?" I asked.

"I went to Sedona that night. I've got bar and hotel receipts, along with a gas receipt for the next morning. I wasn't around."

"You saved your receipts for that night?" I asked, not believing it.

"Heck, yes. They make great kindling for the fire out by Mike and my trailers. Haven't used them yet."

Well, color me surprised.

"I didn't have anything to do with Phoebe dying, and right now, I'm being hired to watch you. I'm totally innocent."

Should I mention that if I wasn't killed, he'd be indicted for kidnapping? Probably not. Best to keep him calm. Apparently, he was too dumb to realize his future.

However, based on the conversation we'd had, I was fairly certain who had killed Phoebe.

And it wasn't Buck.

His phone buzzed in his pocket. After pulling it out, he stood and exited the stall. I strained to hear the conversation, but it seemed he'd stepped outside the barn.

This was my chance to find something that would cut my ropes. I scooted over to my right and continued my exploration of the wall behind me. Nothing. Panic tightened my chest as sweat dripped from my brow. This was a barn, built with nails. Surely there had to be one exposed!

Now desperate, I moved again. Something scratched against my head and I bit my tongue to keep from yelping. I glanced up to find just what I was looking for—a nail.

As a trickle of blood cascaded down the side of my cheek, I made a mental note to get a tetanus shot.

I struggled to my feet. Once I stood, I had to squat down a bit for my hands to reach the nail. After I located it, I rubbed the ropes around my hands against it while I kept an eye on the stall door and concentrated on listening for Buck's return.

A few moments later, I probed my ropes with my fingertips. I wasn't making any progress. With a curse, I leaned against the wall, tears of desperation rolling down my face. At some point, Buck or the person who hired him had to realize that if I was allowed to live, they'd go to prison. Once that happened, it would be lights out for me… permanently.

"Gina! Giiinnna!"

With a gasp, I stilled. Through my drug-soaked brain, I thought I heard Daisy yelling for me.

How would she know where I was? And she hadn't been speaking to me lately, so I wasn't sure if she ever had.

Didn't people hallucinate on opioids? That must've been my issue.

I continued to work the ropes against the nail as sweat joined the blood running down the side of my face.

"Gina! Gina!"

The childlike voice seemed to be getting closer.

"Please be real," I whispered. "Please be real."

I couldn't call out for her. However, I hoped with the amount I was sweating she'd be able to track my scent.

If I wasn't imagining it all.

I listened intently. Did I hear sniffing on the outside of the barn?

A few moments later, I swallowed a scream as something white and brown flew over the door into my stall.

"Gina! Oh my gosh, Gina! What are you doing? Why haven't you come home?!"

Sobs wracked my body as I sank to my knees. Daisy licked away the tears faster than they could fall.

"Ew," she said, stepping away. "That's blood. You taste gross!"

I remembered I was being held hostage... and I wouldn't put her in danger no matter how thrilled I was to see her. "You need to get out of here," I whispered.

"No! I can't!" Daisy yelled. She threw her head back and let out the longest, loudest howl I'd ever heard.

Running footsteps sounded from outside. A second later, Buck burst into the stall. He glanced from me to Daisy.

"Go!" I yelled as he picked up the shovel.

Daisy bared her teeth and turned to him. Placing herself in between me and my kidnapper, she lowered herself into an attack position and growled.

CHAPTER 20

BUCK RAISED the shovel over his head as he yelled, "Where did the dog come from?!"

I realized he was going to try to hurt Daisy.

"No!" I yelled. Without considering the consequences, I lunged at him just as he brought the shovel down. It missed me by inches while my shoulder connected with his gut. I heard the shovel toppling to the ground behind me as I continued my run at Buck. Daisy growled and barked incessantly while I screamed. He was too big to send over my shoulder as I'd done with Debbie, but I also didn't have use of my hands. I ran on pure adrenaline, fear and anger.

Buck yelled at me, but I had shut my eyes and kept my shoulder connected to him. No one hurt my dog. No one. If they tried, they'd pay the price, and it was a hefty one.

There had to be another stall or wall behind him somewhere. And when he finally hit it, I had plans for planting my foot in his nether region.

When I landed face-first in the dirt, my mind spun with confusion. Where the heck had he gone? He'd pulled some magical Harry Potter move on me or something, but I quickly flipped to my back and brought my legs up, ready for attack—

Vic.

My brother had Buck in a chokehold. "You'd better be happy I've got the police here with me," he whispered, "or I'd take you out back and make sure they never found your remains again. You *don't* mess with my sister, Buck."

I turned to the door and spotted

Trevor and Sheriff Mallory running with the Wagners and Chase not far behind. Trevor hurried to my side and helped me to my feet, then suddenly, my hands were free. I heard the *snap* of his pocketknife closing.

As Daisy trotted over to me, I dropped to my knees and gathered her into my arms. I didn't know the details of how she'd found me, but I'd ask later. I'd never been so relieved to see anyone.

"What the heck is going on here?" Roger boomed.

Unfortunately, I had a pretty good idea.

I stood to my full height with my dog at my feet and rubbed my wrists while stretching out my fingers, just in case I needed to punch someone. I liked to be prepared.

"We're finding Phoebe's killer," I announced.

"The killer's been found," Roger said, lifting his chin defiantly. "He's standing right in front of us." His gaze drifted over to Vic, who'd pushed Buck to the ground.

"We all know that's a lie," I snapped.

"What's a lie?" Chase asked. "I thought it was certain that Vic killed her! Why isn't he behind bars?"

"Our sheriff has been quite mistaken in where she places her guilt," I said, leaving out the part that she was also lazy and would throw her own mother in prison if she could make it fit her own narrative.

"Evidence doesn't lie," Mallory said. "And I have all the evidence I need."

"Not true," I replied, then turned to Trevor. "What did the cameras show?"

"Cameras?" Mallory said, her brow furrowed. "What's this about cameras?"

"There are cameras all over the property, ma'am," Trevor replied. "We were never told of their existence and I believe this may be the key to solving the case. I've got a warrant for the footage."

She glared at him, then at me. Daisy was walking around sniffing everyone's shoes. I had a good idea of who'd actually killed Phoebe, but if Daisy could confirm it for me, that would be great. I just needed to keep everyone talking for a few moments.

"Whose dog is this?" Cynthia asked, moving away from her.

"She's mine," I said.

"Why are you in my barn with this... this man?" Cynthia continued, pointing at Buck.

"He kidnapped me from the grocery store and brought me here," I replied. I turned my stare to Mallory. "And I'd like to press charges, if it's not too much trouble."

Her cheeks reddened and I smiled. More paperwork for the laziest sheriff in history? She wasn't happy.

"I'll make sure Buck gets booked," Trevor said. "Don't worry about that, Gina."

I smiled and nodded, glad I could count on my new friend to have my back.

"Why in the world would he do that?" Cynthia asked, confusion lacing her voice. If I read her correctly, she truly didn't know what was happening.

I glanced around and said, "The three of you all gained something by Phoebe's death." I pointed at the Wagners and Chase. "But then there's Buck here. He's stupid enough to do something horrible if there's enough money involved."

"Hey!" he yelled. "I told you, I didn't have anything to do with it!"

"Shut up," Trevor growled.

"I gained nothing by her death," Cynthia sniffed, crossing her arms over her chest. "We *lost* one of our best trainers."

"Of course you benefited from Phoebe dying," I said. "Your husband's girlfriend was out of the picture."

Cynthia narrowed her gaze, then shot her husband a glare. "That may be the case, but I'd never kill her."

"I figured as much," I sighed. "Because why would you kill your husband's girlfriend when you've got a little side piece yourself? Unless you believe you're the only one who should get to play around."

Chase's cheeks turned the color of apples while Daisy sniffed around his feet. I wanted to speak with her, to tell her to hurry and tell me about the third person she smelled in the horse ring the day Phoebe was killed.

"What in the world?" Roger whispered while Cynthia stared at her shoes where Daisy was taking an interest.

"Why is this dog sniffing my feet?" she muttered, pushing Daisy's nose with her foot.

"Leave her be," I said. "She's not bothering you, but if you hurt her, I will be the biggest pain you've ever had." I turned my attention to Chase. "And you… with Phoebe gone, you got your big promotion that you believe should've been yours."

"Yes, but I would never kill her—or anyone for that matter—even if the promotion was unfair."

"And why was it unfair?" I asked.

His gaze bounced from me to Roger. "The boss was sleeping with Phoebe, and I was more qualified for the position than her. It should've gone to me to begin with."

Cynthia's face turned ashen but kept

her facial features neutral. Maybe she hadn't known her husband's infidelity wasn't top secret?

"But with her out of the way, you slid right into the position," I countered. "How convenient for you!"

"I didn't kill her!" Chase shouted. "You aren't going to pin this on me!"

Daisy trotted over to Roger. It only took a second before she started yelling. "It's him! Gina, It's him! Should I bite his ankles?"

Shaking my head, I turned to the owner of Diamond Ranch. I had Daisy's confirmation that he was the one she'd smelled in the horse arena. How did I prove it without telling everyone my talking dog was how speaking to me after a long hiatus where I'd thought my mind had somehow returned to normal?

"Roger, it must've been difficult for you to have Phoebe breakup with you," I said softly. "Did it throw you into a fit of rage?"

He stared at me silently, his nostrils flaring.

"And you must have seen the texts between Vic and her when you broke into her phone. She'd never written anything like that to you, had she?"

His gaze shifted to above my head. He wouldn't meet my stare.

"Here's my guess," I said, hoping to get at least some of this mess right. "Vic met with Phoebe that night in the arena. Maybe you even saw it on camera… if the cameras were working, of course. You went out after and talked to her after Vic left. She told you that it was over. Maybe you even questioned her about her relationship with Vic. After the chat, you left the arena but came back once she was done training the horse. You snuck up on her and took a pipe to the back of her head, leaving her in the middle of the arena to die while you took the horse back to its stall."

Cynthia gasped. "Roger! Did you do this?"

"Of course not," he growled. "This is all conjecture. There's no proof of any of it."

"What about the cameras?" she shrieked. "They'll show everything!"

"The cameras are broken again," he said, a small smile playing on his lips. "I have to call to have them repaired."

"Actually, I worked on the system the day Phoebe was killed," Chase said. "I got it back up and running that afternoon."

The color drained from Roger's face.

"Give me your phone," I demanded from Trevor, wondering where mine had gone. Maybe sitting in the trunk of my car with all my groceries that had most likely gone bad?

He handed it over and I dialed the burner phone number I'd committed to memory.

I waited for it to connect, then a ringing sounded from Buck's direction.

We all stared at him. "That's the phone he used to send the texts, pretending to be Vic," I said, turning to Trevor. "I dialed that number. Remember, you couldn't find who it belonged to."

Vic bent over and searched Buck's

pockets. A moment later, he pulled out the phone and held it out in front of him.

"It's not mine!" Buck yelled, then he pointed at Roger. "He gave it to me to carry! Said he'd pay me fifty bucks to keep it with me at all times!"

Roger paled further, then ran for the door. Before any of us could register that we needed to chase him, Daisy barked and followed at top speed. She hurried past him, then put herself between Roger and the door, baring her teeth and growling. I'd never seen my sweet girl look so fierce.

"Get away!" Roger yelled, trying to juke around her. "Move!"

Trevor and Vic both pursued him. Vic tackled him from behind and straddled his back. As Roger squirmed and yelled, Trevor slapped a pair of handcuffs over his wrists and began reciting his Miranda rights.

Daisy trotted over to me and I fell to my knees, taking her into a tight embrace.

"We did it, Gina!" Daisy whispered in my ear. "We found who killed Phoebe!

Now you'll have time to take me for walks!"

I chuckled as I buried my head next to her ear. Of course at first I did suspect she'd quit talking to me when I didn't have time to take her for her walks—but then I had started believing all this talking to dogs stuff had been in my head. Turned out my initial gut feeling had been right. We'd need to have a discussion about that.

Once Roger was contained, Vic stormed over to Buck, standing over him with his fists at his sides and his nostrils flaring.

"You want to tell me what you were doing holding my sister hostage?" he asked.

"R-Roger called me from the grocery store," he stammered. "Told me he'd pay me a thousand dollars to take Gina and hide her in the barn. I had no idea why or what was going on. I just need the money. Someone changed the locks on my trailer. Mike's, too. We busted down the doors, but..."

His voice trailed off. Someone changed the locks on his trailer? Who would do such a thing, and why?

Buck had proven once again that he was stupid enough to be dangerous.

"I still want him arrested for kidnapping," I said loudly, pointing at him.

Trevor nodded. "Yes, ma'am."

"And Buck, I want to know what the warning was that you gave Vic because he owed you money," I said through gritted teeth.

"There wasn't one," he muttered. "We were just trying to scare you so we'd get paid."

"I also want him in jail for threatening me," I said to Trevor.

"Will do, Gina. I'll make sure he gets the full weight of the law thrown at him."

Feeling somewhat satisfied, but still shaky and upset, I glanced over at the sheriff, who simply stared at Roger Wagner. I expected her to say something. Maybe a thank you for solving Phoebe's murder was in order? Or, I'm sorry you were kidnapped and drugged? When she wouldn't meet my gaze I turned to Vic. "Let's go home."

He led me over to my car and I slid into the passenger seat after Daisy jumped into the back.

Soon, we were driving away from Diamond Ranch and relief swept through me.

"How did you know where I was?" I asked.

"I didn't," he replied. "When you didn't come home from the grocery store, I called Trevor. He was already at the ranch and told me to come out. Your friend in back insisted on coming with me. Wouldn't take no for an answer. I tried everything to get her back into the house, but then I just let her in the car."

"If you were at the ranch, I wanted to help find you!" Daisy exclaimed. "I knew I could do it with my super sniffer!"

I reached back and scratched under her chin. Thank goodness for her super sniffer. Not only had it found me, but she'd also helped me pinpoint who had killed Phoebe.

Still exhausted, I laid my head back against the headrest. As I drifted off to sleep, I imagined the moment Jacob would walk through the door.

My heart filled with love as tears pricked my eyes. I couldn't wait to see my kid.

CHAPTER 21

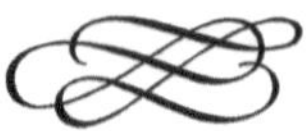

FRIDAY ROLLED AROUND and I kept an eye on the clock as I half-listened to my customers at File It Away. Daisy spent most of the day staring out the front door.

"Is he coming here?" she asked. "I want to see Jacob! He always plays chase with me!"

I didn't bother to remind her again that Jacob would be dropped at the house.

Just as I was finishing up, Annabelle walked in with her beagle, Jack. Daisy and Jack sniffed each other while Annabelle gave me a hug.

"Oh, my gosh, Gina," she said. "I heard what happened to you. That's, like, crazy."

"I know," I sighed, wondering if I'd ever get used to her affection. "It was scary."

She pushed her kinked hair over her shoulder, her bracelets rattling up and down her arm. Today she wore black and pink biking shorts with an oversized white t-shirt that read, *Relax, Don't Do It* tied in a knot at her waist. Black eyeliner lined her eyes, and she'd gone a little heavy on the pink blush. "Well, at least Buck got a little taste of his own medicine." A small smile crept across her face while I furrowed my brow.

Then I realized what she meant. "You changed the locks on their trailers?"

"Maybe I did, maybe I didn't," she said. "But revenge is sweet, isn't it?"

I burst out laughing. Perhaps I'd even feel bad for the two if Buck hadn't kidnapped me and held me hostage in a barn.

We chatted for a few more minutes and I invited her to say hello to Jacob over the weekend.

"How's he doing?" she asked. "Is he liking college?"

"He's coming home to escape party central," I replied. "So, I think he does enjoy it, but just needs a little break."

After Annabelle left, Daisy and I hurried home to get some work done on my new mystery book. I really hoped the author liked it. The words had come much easier than they had for the space romance, mainly because I was simply writing about my own experience. The chapter where the main character was trapped in a barn still angered when I read it. Annabelle may have changed his locks in her tit-for-tat over them threatening me, but I hoped Buck would be in jail for a very long time for what he did. Dumb or not, he'd scared me to death and I wanted him to pay for it.

My groceries had been ruined sitting in the summer sun when Buck grabbed me, so Vic had been kind enough to head back to the store and fetch everything on my list. For the first time in months, I was having an old-fashioned barbecue with my whole family.

When we got together, I often wondered what had happened to my mother. Was she alive? Dead? Had Vic and I really been such horrible children that she couldn't put up with us anymore? Or had she ran from my father? If so, why? The questions plagued me. Yes, I'd asked them, but I'd never received a real answer. Maybe Mom was the only one who could tell us the truth, and frankly, I wasn't sure I wanted to hear it.

"Is he here?" Daisy asked from the back seat as we pulled into the driveway. "Is he here?"

I briefly studied the house. Now that Vic was in the clear, we'd opened the blinds, but I didn't see any movement inside. "If he's not here, he will be soon," I replied as my heart skipped a beat. I couldn't wait to get my hands on my kid.

We exited the car and Daisy ran up to the front door, her nose to the ground while her tail wagged. "He's here!" she yelled. "Open the door! Open it!"

Her excitement was contagious as we stepped inside. "Jacob?" I yelled.

"I'm out back, Mom!"

After setting down my bag, I took a deep breath hoping to calm the butterflies in my belly. For some reason, I didn't want him to know I desperately missed him. Probably because he'd feel guilty and I didn't want to put that on him. It was time for him to spread his wings and fly. He didn't need me to tie him down.

I hurried into the kitchen to find my son coming inside. Banshee sat at the feeding bowls and eyed me with disdain, which I assumed was because the bowls were empty.

With a smile, Jacob held his hands wide and I wrapped my arms around his waist. Tears came to my eyes as he embraced me.

"I'm so glad to see you," I whispered.

"Glad to be home, Mom," he said.

After pulling away, I gave him a quick study. Two arms, two legs. Had he dropped a bit of weight? Was he growing his hair out, or had he not had time for a haircut? The light purple rings under his eyes indicated he was a bit tired, but over-all, he looked good. Relief swelled through me and I smiled. Would I ever quit worrying about him? Probably not.

"Chase me, Jacob!" Daisy yelled. "Chase me! I bet you can't catch me!" She stared up at him with her tail wagging and her ears perked.

"In a little bit," I said, leaning over and kissing her nose. "Give him some time to get settled."

"Aww…. Darn it! I want to play now!"

"I swear you can talk to that dog," Jacob said, laughing. "What does she want? For me to chase her?"

"You're absolutely correct," I said, standing to my full height and giving him a wink. "Maybe you're the one who's learning to speak to the puppies."

I glanced behind him. Vic and my father were sitting outside at the small table on my patio sharing a bottle of Scotch.

Both waved. Vic slowly moved his hand over Sing's head. The dog's eyes were half-closed, his tongue lolling out the side of his mouth. He seemed quite content.

"Hey," I said, wishing I'd remember to water the darn petunias. My little patio area would be so cute if the flowers weren't struggling so much.

"Hi, Gina," my father said. As I leaned over and kissed his cheek, his gray beard scratched my chin. "Vic was just telling us about your adventures this week."

"It's been a rough one," I said. "But at least Vic isn't going to jail for something he didn't do."

"Yes," my dad replied. "Thank you for standing by him."

"He didn't make it easy," I muttered.

"He never does, honey," my father chuckled. "He never does."

"Mom, you're so cool," Jacob exclaimed as we sat down. Daisy sighed and curled at my feet. "Vic said you were just awesome."

I arched an eyebrow at my brother. "Oh, really?"

"Sure you were," he said, crossing his arms over his chest as he leaned back in the chair so it balanced on the rear two legs. I kind of hoped he'd tip over. "It was a rough week, but everything turned out okay. For me, at least. Not for Phoebe, though."

A heavy silence fell over us. Maybe Phoebe would be with us right now if not for Roger. I hoped he got what he deserved in prison.

"Anyway," Vic said, "Cynthia called me today. She wants me to come back as top trainer."

Finally, I'd get my brother out of my hair. But then, I'd also miss having him around a little bit. "That's great news," I said. "You better keep yourself in line, though."

"I will. I think I've finally learned my lesson."

My father snorted as I rolled my eyes. "Where have I heard that before?" I asked.

Vic laughed. "This time, I mean it. And, I was wondering if I could take you up on that offer and have my buddy move in with me."

His buddy. He glanced down at the chow sitting next to him. Well, be still my beating heart. "You want Sing?"

"Yeah," Vic said with a goofy grin. "He's grown on me. I like the dude."

Sing's tail slowly moved back and forth as he eyed me.

"I think that's a really good match," I said. "Make sure to take good care of him."

"I will. I think he'll like the ranch."

"I think he'll like your couch," Daisy muttered.

"Tell us about your schooling, son," my dad interjected. "What are those communists at the college filling your head with?"

"I'll get the barbeque fired up," Vic said. "I'm starving."

As Jacob talked about his classes, I glanced around the table. This was my family. For better or worse, they belonged to me, and I appreciated and loved them, even if Vic did get on my last nerve.

EPILOGUE

As summer faded and fall slowly moved in, the leaves on the trees along the river began to turn beautiful shades of red, yellow and orange. Even though I'd lived in Heywood my whole life, I never tired of seeing them and each year I was awestruck by their beauty.

As Daisy and I walked along the River-walk in the crisp morning hours, she chatted incessantly about a cat we'd seen earlier while I admired the trees and thought about my day. I had completed the murder mystery book and turned it in to the author, who had loved it and commissioned another one. I had no plot, so my mind seemed to continuously spin with ideas.

"I think that cat wanted to eat me," Daisy said. "Either that, or beat me up. He was not a nice cat."

The feline had come out from behind a bush, then hissed and snarled at us. Daisy barked, and the two engaged in a standoff until I finally pulled her leash and we moved past it. I assumed the cat to be feral, so I debated whether to call a rescue organization or not. I didn't take in cats, but others in the area did. However, the cat had looked very well fed and healthy, so perhaps he was simply out and about for a morning stroll, just like us.

My phone buzzed in my pocket, and I pulled it out. Sally from On The River. What in the world could she want? We were friends, but we rarely spoke on the phone.

"Hi, Sally," I said. "What's up?"

"Gina?" she sniffled. "I'm sorry, I don't know who else to call."

"What's wrong?" I asked as dread weighed in my chest. "Are you crying?"

"I came in to open the restaurant," she whispered. "And… and one of my workers is dead."

"Who is it?"

"One of my chefs. Mario."

As I stopped walking, I furrowed my brow. "Well, you may want to call an ambulance." I said. "Maybe he isn't dead. Maybe he had a heart attack or something."

"No, he was murdered, Gina. He's got my favorite knife sticking out of his chest."

"Oh, my word," I whispered. "Have you called the police?"

"Yes. They're here now."

"You need a lawyer," I said. "And you need to keep your mouth shut."

"It's too late."

"What does that mean?" I asked.

"I was nervous… I told Mallory and Trevor that it was my favorite knife and that I'd had an argument with him before I left last night, and I was the last to see him alive."

My heart sank as dread filled my stomach. I needed to sit down. Daisy still prattled on about the cat. My lovely morning had turned ugly.

"Please come help me, Gina. I'm really afraid of what's going to happen. They keep asking me all these questions… I'm scared they're going to pin this on me like they did to Vic about Phoebe's death."

I shut my eyes and rubbed my hand over my forehead. No way was I allowing my friend to take the fall for her dead chef.

I'd simply have to find the real killer myself.

WHAT DARK SECRETS does the victim have in his past? Will Gina be able to help Sally find the real killer? Find out in Paw Prints and Problems.

Bernie and the ghost of her dead grandmother find themselves in the middle of various murder investigations. Danger and hilarity ensues as the crazy duo follow the clues to discover the killers.

The Tri-Town Murders

(Small town contemporary cozies)

Complete Series

Follow newspaper reporter Tilly and her group of fun, quirky friends as they solve murders in a fictional, small town in California.

Killer Skies Mysteries

Set in 1965, join Patty Briggs, stewardess extraordinaire, as she flies the skies and solves murders with the help of her friends… and one cute FBI agent!

ABOUT THE AUTHOR

USA Today bestselling author Carly Winter writes fun, small town cozy mysteries, always with a dash of humor and quirky characters. When not writing, you can find her spending time with her family, on a Pilates reformer or enjoying the fantastic Arizona weather (except summer - she doesn't like summer). She does like dogs, wine and chocolate and wishes Christmas happened twice a year.

For more information on her books, please visit: CarlyWinterCozyMysteries.com